Secrets and Lies

Jacquelyn Johnson

Cataloguing in Publication Data

Jacquelyn Johnson

Secrets and Lies

Description: Crimson Hill Books trade paperback edition | Nova Scotia, Canada

ISBN:	978-1-990291-63-0 (Paperback – Draft2Digital)
BISAC:	YAF000000 Young Adult Fiction: General YAF022000 Young Adult Fiction: Girls & Women YAF058020 Young Adult Fiction: Social Themes – Bullying
THEMA:	FXB – Narrative Theme: Coming of age YXO -- Children's / Teenage personal & social issues: Bullying, violence, abuse & peer pressure YXHB -- Children's / Teenage personal & social issues: Friends & friendship issues

Record available at https://www.bac-lac.gc.ca/eng/Pages/home.aspx

Front Cover Image: Cristina Zabolotnii

Book Design & Formatting: Jesse Johnson

Gus sings a few lines from Octopus's Garden by Richard Starkey (Ringo Starr) ©Starling Music Ltd.

Crimson Hill Books
(a division of)
Crimson Hill Products Inc.
Wolfville, Nova Scotia
Canada

Crimson Hill
Books

Sam Park, Morley's best friend, has suddenly moved away without a word of warning. She's just – gone.

A long-awaited vacation with her favourite aunt is cancelled at the last minute. No one will say why.

And where is her real father? Why is everything about him still such a mystery? Why won't her mother tell her anything at all about the Dad she longs to know?

Morley Star isn't just disappointed. She feels angry, lied to, left out and betrayed.

As she searches for answers, secrets are, at last, revealed. But could it be that the biggest lies are the ones Morley is telling herself?

Fifth in the Morley Stories series of novels for girls ages 10 to 13. While this book is part of a series, it is also a complete, standalone story.

Also In
The Morley Stories
Series:

Just Me. Morley

Feather's Girl

Gifted

Rules for Flying

Secrets and Lies

Sisters

Find them all at
www.CrimsonHillBooks.com

Is your glass half-empty, or half-full? Only you

can decide.

Gus Ferguson

A Little Note on Names:

Irish names don't look anything like you might think they sound unless you're Irish. Here's how to say these names correctly for all the rest of us who just wish we could sound like we're Irish:

Aoife is a very popular name in Ireland. It means beautiful and joyful. It sounds like this: EEEE-fa

Sorcha means bright. Say it like this: SUR-ka

Eire, short for Eireann, means Ireland. Say it like this: EYE-ra

one

I race down the stairs just in time to see the ride-share car pulling away.

"Good-bye," Sam shouts from the back seat, her words grabbed right out of her mouth by the winter wind.

Call me I gesture as they drive away.

Until just a few minutes ago, we were sitting on the rug in the living room with beads and findings, wire and silk cord spread all around us, making bracelets, snacking on treats and laughing.

I knew Sam's mother was coming. I just hoped it would take Ms. Park longer to get here. Or, even better, maybe she'd never show up at all.

Shivering, I follow Aunt Eira back into the house. When I've got the jewellery stuff put away, I head out to the kitchen with our empty treat plates and glasses.

Green for Sam, her favourite colour. Red for me.

Sam and Umma, that's what she calls her mother, are headed for New York City. That's where Sam goes this time every year to get a lesson with Madame Belanger. Madame is a famous music teacher from Paris. You need to be brilliant to get to work with Madame.

Sam plays piano and violin. Not like the way most kids who take music lessons can play. More like a real musician that you would see at a symphony concert. *Gifted*, is what they call Sam. I just call her my best friend who likes music. And school. And pets. And just hanging out together with me and, sometimes, our other best friend, Jayden. This doesn't happen as often as I'd like.

Sam could've waited just one more minute until I got downstairs to say good-bye. That's what I thought she'd do. I wanted to hug her. Wish her Good Luck. Say, "Have a great time in New York and I'll see you really soon."

But no. Her mother has suddenly turned up and swept her off to the airport.

It's not as if I didn't know our holiday together was going to end. I can't ever remember a time when I felt so free to just be myself, the real me. Like life is exactly the way it's supposed to be, which is happy.

I get how lucky I am. I do. This crazy, accidental Christmas has been the very best week of my life. Now, it feels like it's over.

Soon my mother will get home with our new baby

sister. Danny will get here to pick up Daisy, who's my little sister. Then Aunt Eira and Dom will go back to their own place.

Life will be back to pretty much the way it always is, with Uncle Gus, me and my mother, except Daisy will be in the city with her dad and we'll have a new little baby.

Lily Holly Noelle Star was born on Christmas Eve. Because of the big winter storm that knocked out the power, I haven't even met her yet, but I'm not expecting much. New little babies sleep all the time. That's what I've heard. They sleep and drink milk and fill up their diapers. That's all they know how to do. Maybe Lily will get more interesting when she turns into an actual kid. I don't know. I've never been where there's a baby before.

No, that's not quite true. I was five when Daisy was born, but I remember hardly anything about way back then except that Danny was with us. He used to be Mom's boyfriend. He's Daisy's father. Lily's, too. Not mine.

Danny moved back to the city last winter, just after Christmas. Mom says they decided they didn't want to be together anymore. I don't think that's the real reason, but in our family there are so many secrets. It's hard to find out anything for sure.

Another big thing that happened is we got rid of the horrible renter people who used to live upstairs. They were always screaming and fighting. Now, upstairs is all fixed up and turned into a bed and breakfast. So that's more work, looking after the guests. I still don't get to have my bedroom back, with my own desk to do art and write stories, because now it's a room for the guests.

A bed and breakfast, if you've never stayed in one, is kind of like an inn. Tourists come to stay overnight, or maybe for a few nights. It's like staying at a hotel. Only nicer, as my Aunt Eira says, because the guests get to be in a real home. They also get breakfast made by Mom. She's amazing at baking things like cranberry scones and cherry Danishes and all sorts of cookies and cakes. The guests go crazy for her baking.

Mom used to be the secretary at our school, but now her job is looking after the bed and breakfast guests and baking cookies and cakes for some of the restaurants around here and to sell at the Saturday market. I help with our market booth and sell what I make. That's bead jewellery and pet portraits.

A couple of months ago, after his house burnt down, Uncle Gus moved in as one of our guests. He also has most of his meals with us. He's not really our uncle, just a friend who likes to think that we're his family. I like that, too.

Now, I'm trying to think about some things to cheer myself up. Making a list in my head.

A few months ago, I got Feather, our little black cat. I started selling my jewellery and drawings of pets, mostly dogs and cats. I got permission to start the Pet Club at school. I started teaching Daisy how to draw. I did a presentation to the pet rescue shelter people about how to get more kids like me involved in helping pets. Those are good things that have happened this year. Most of them.

Christmas, this Christmas, with just my favourite people at our house, was the very best thing to happen this year. So far. There's only a few more days before it turns into next year, so I think probably that's going to stay true, but you never know. That's what Gus is always saying.

"Anything could happen," is one of his favourite old-timey sayings. I guess that's right. Anything could happen, even in boring old Seabright, where we live. Even something that's a total surprise. Just look at this Christmas and how different it turned out to be than anybody could have expected.

Christmas vacation always starts with my sleepover. It's always on the very last day of school before vacation. Except this year, on that night, there was this crazy huge winter storm.

If you live on the seashore, or close, like we do, storms that come roaring up the coast, ripping up houses and boats and tossing everything around, are nothing new. Nor'easters happen just about every year.

On the news they said the Nor'easter was coming, but everyone was surprised by how fast it got here and how fierce it was. We had to stop my sleepover party only a couple hours after it got started. Everybody had to go home because their parents were worried about them.

Sam was the only one who didn't leave. I guess her mother got stuck in the city or somewhere. Their housekeeper, Margaret, had already left to spend

Christmas with her own family down in Mexico.
Margaret got on her plane and was far away and safe
when the storm hit here. I know Sam was relieved
about that, but it also meant she didn't have anyone
to come pick her up.

I'm not sure why her mother was the only parent who
didn't turn up to get their daughter on sleepover
night. Sam didn't want to say, but I also know that
her mom didn't even answer her phone or texts. Sam
and I ended up having our own besties sleepover, just
the two of us, which was fun. After that, we still didn't
hear from her mom, so she stayed with us for all of
Christmas week, up til today. December 27.

Yesterday morning, the power knocked out by the
storm finally came back on. After the storm stopped
blowing and headed out to sea, like it usually does, all
the neighbours got out with their chain saws to clear
the trees that came crashing down. We helped. It was
kind of fun, like a street party.

On the news they reported that everywhere, from New
York to here, everyone was doing the same thing.
That is getting broken trees and damaged cars out of
the way, working along with the emergency crews.
Once the trees and downed power lines and the rest of
the wreckage were gone, it was possible to open the
roads again.

Christmas at our house wasn't a huge crowd of family,
like it is most other years. It was just three adults and
three kids. Uncle Gus, Aunt Eira and her fiancé, Dom
and Daisy, Sam and me. Oh, and the cats, my Feather
and Eira's little gray Bengal who's called Pixel.

Cats can't eat turkey or any other Christmas food. They liked playing with the gift wrap, though, and batting at the ornaments on the tree. And trying to climb up it.

Our other aunt, Sorcha, and her husband and their two little boys were supposed to be here for Christmas, too, but the storm meant they stayed home. Aunt Eira and Dom were already here. They came to help with my sleepover party. Then, they stayed to look after Daisy and me while Mom was in hospital having Lily. Mom thought she and Lily would be back home way before Christmas day, but that didn't happen.

Aunt Sorcha is a nurse. One of the things she told me is babies are born when they're ready to be born. Usually that's at night. It might not be the exact night you think they'll arrive. Good to know, I guess, if I ever decide to be a mother. Maybe I will, but not for a long time. After I've gotten to travel and study art. And maybe live in some other countries. Just to see what that would be like.

A couple of hours ago, Mom called and said she'll be allowed home today with Lily. Our special Christmas present is what Mom calls our new baby sister, but I already know what my special Christmas present was. It was that feeling of being really, truly happy and not worried about anything. I think about this and sort of try to hug that feeling to me, not ever wanting to let it go.

I guess Mom really means Lily is HER special gift, because I know Daisy didn't ask for another kid in our family. Neither did I.

What my mother doesn't know, yet, but I guess she's going to notice soon, is that Aunt Eira and Dom gave me a laptop AND a phone for Christmas. And not only that – they paid for my phone service for a whole year and for a year of WIFI. I was just about the only kid in grade 6 who didn't have a phone. Or a computer at home. Really fantastic gifts, I was totally surprised! Especially since there's a no-computers-for-kids rule in our house and my mother said I couldn't have a phone until I pay for it myself. So, I don't know if she's going to take my phone and laptop away. At least I've got them right now. For as long as it takes before she finds out. I've told her about needing a phone to stay in touch and be safe and I need a laptop to do my schoolwork, but she just doesn't listen.

Maybe she'll be so busy with the baby, she won't even notice. Hope so.

I pull my new phone out of my back pocket and send a text to Sam: *Sorry. Wanted to say bye. For now. And Good Luck!* I give it a smiley.

Then I text my other best friend, Jayden: *Sam just left.* I add a face with big fat tears.

Jayden texts back in seconds. *Yeah, but back soon. Aren't you going away 2, this weeknd?* He's added a happy face.

Yes. Just 4 more days. How r you? How was Christmas? I text back.

Awesome. Totally. Gotta go. Patrick waiting. Catch ya latr.

Patrick is 18 and Jayden's favourite brother. He's the

one who breeds and trains horses and the one who taught Sam and me how to ride.

I wait a bit, but there's no reply from Sam. Then I go find my aunt, who must think I look kind of droopy, because she says, "It was a great Christmas we had together, wasn't it? And soon, it will be you and me leaving for the airport! Aren't you excited? I am!"

She's right. Just a few days from now, I'll give Gus and then Feather a big hug good-bye. Then it'll be my turn to get in a taxi going to the airport and towards an adventure in a big city. One of the biggest – New York! Mom tried to say I couldn't go, but Aunt Eira talked her into it and I'm grateful.

When I close my eyes, I can almost hear the city traffic sounds and feel what it's going to be like to walk into *Wicked*, the show we're going to see. Or order absolutely anything I want to eat with no mother rules. Or just hang out with Eira. She's my aunt and my mother's youngest sister. The fun one.

I like to pretend Eira is my mother, not my aunt. Maybe there was some kind of mix up. Or, I don't know, just a mistake. Even if that would be a strange kind of mistake. I wish it wasn't just a story I like to tell myself, that Eira is my mum, and the mother I live with is just my aunt. Or not even related to me.

If there was anything I could do to make this true, I would. But you don't get to pick your family. Just your friends.

We'll be going shopping and to restaurants and parks and museums and on a boat tour and a city tour. They're all the cool things Sam gets to do, when she goes to New York City every year with her mother. She always tells me all about it when she gets back, right before school starts up again. I hear about restaurants with all kinds of different foods to try out. Art galleries with so many rooms on so many floors, you can't possibly see everything. Museums that are the same, full of amazing stuff. Travelling on the subway, going to the top of the Empire State Building, riding on the ferry or taking an evening boat tour around Manhattan, going to stores that have every single thing you could dream of wanting in every size and every colour...and, even better, all the different kinds of people there are.

It always makes me jealous, hearing about all the fun things Sam gets to see and do while I'm just back home doing all the same old stupid boring stuff. I always hoped I'd get invited to go to New York with Sam and her mother. I did a LOT of hinting, but they never invited me.

I finally get to go there and see all that. With just Aunt Eira and me. It will be the very first time I've ever been that far away from home. The very first time I've been in a place that large. It's going to be almost five whole glorious days with just the two of us, my favourite adult in the whole world and me, doing whatever we feel like doing. And seeing. And eating.

We might even meet up with Sam and her mother there. That would be cool.

I can hardly wait!

two

Here's a secret I know about my little sister, Daisy. When she goes to the city with her dad this week, one of the things that's going to happen is she's getting a hearing test. I'm pretty sure she's not going to like somebody poking around in her ears and figuring out if something's wrong. She doesn't usually like anyone touching her, especially strangers like a doctor or nurse. Danny made the appointment with the ear specialist, Aunt Eira told me. It's going to happen.

I never even thought that maybe Daisy's hearing isn't just like everyone else's. I just thought she's a really LOUD little kid, always making some kind of stupid noise. She never really notices what you say to her unless you're looking right at her, and she can't ignore you.

Mom says Daisy "only hears things when she wants to." I guess that's what we all thought.

I feel bad about it now. I'm sorry about the times I wasn't very nice to her. If she really can't hear, it isn't her fault.

It was Sam who noticed first. She played a kind of music game on the piano – well, Daisy thought it was just a game. Really it was more than that, because Daisy couldn't hear playing softly when everyone else in the room could. As we watched Sam and Daisy playing the piano game, we all knew that something was wrong.

We didn't say anything, at least not right then when Daisy was there and all happy, playing the game with Sam. It would have scared her.

I think Aunt Eira and Dom and Gus were shocked when Sam's game showed us how Daisy couldn't hear. I sure was.

I don't know if anyone's told my mom about the piano game yet. Probably Aunt Eira has. I'm glad it doesn't have to be me telling Mom. She'd just say, "Don't be ridiculous. Stop telling tales, Morley! There's nothing wrong with your sister!"

Once Sam showed us, it makes sense that really, Daisy isn't just being bratty and ignoring us or shouting instead of talking. Now that I think about it, her talking is kind of babyish for a kid who's 7. If she really can't hear very well, that would maybe explain why. Aunt Eira told me it might mean Daisy has to learn how to use a hearing aid.

I find Daisy sitting at the kitchen table, colouring pictures of mermaids and fairies that I drew for her. Mom says we need to make presents, not just buy people something at the store. She says the gifts you make mean more than ones you just go out and pay money for. The gift I made for Daisy, one of them, was a book of my drawings of fairies and mermaids for her to colour.

Aunt Eira is frying chunks of beef and cutting up vegetables and putting them in the crockpot for a stew for dinner. She says she doesn't need any help. Dom and Gus have gone to fetch Mom and Lily and bring them home. Danny emailed to say he's on his way.

"Hey, Daisy," I say, sitting down next to her. She tries to ignore me. "Be quiet, Morley," she says in her serious voice. "I have to do colouring right now!"

Aunt Eira laughs. Daisy doesn't notice.

I sit across from Daisy. I lean in towards her and say, "I know something special about mermaids."

"No, you don't." She goes back to her picture, giving the mermaid pink glitter hair.

Gently, I touch her cheek, and this makes her look up. "I do," I say. "But it's a secret."

She looks wary, but also kind of interested. "It can't be a secret because I'm a fairy and my real name is Fae," she says. "I already know every single thing about fairies. AND mermaids!"

"But Fae," I say, "do you know every single thing about the fairies who know how to turn into mermaids?"

She looks doubtful. "Fairies can't turn into mermaids.

They're always fairies," she says. "Go away, Morley. Leave me alone!"

I sense Aunt Eira almost saying something but stopping herself. I try again. "Well, this is really, really secret, but there are some mermaids that DO know how to change into fairies. Really special mermaids. AND these mermaid- fairies, when they're in the ocean they can listen to the fishes sing."

This gets her attention. She's staring at me now. Suddenly, I realize she's reading my lips. I'm sure of it. How did I never notice this before? How come nobody did?

"Fishes...?" she says. It sounds more like fih-hiz. That's another thing that I guess should have been a big clue about Daisy's hearing. She used to speak more clearly.

"Fishes that sing beautiful songs. Only other fishes can ever hear their magical songs. And mermaids, the special ones who are fairy mermaids."

"Oh," she says, sighing. "Like me?"

"Just like you," I say. "But you know, they can't ever hear the fishes sing, or the whales whisper, or the octopuses telling their strange stories about the deepest, darkest and most secret places in the ocean, or the whales' stories about their great journeys across all the oceans of the world, unless they have a magic seashell. It's a special little shell the fairy mermaids wear over their ear, all pink and pearly."

"Oh..." Daisy says. "Like the big shell we hold up to our ear, to hear the ocean roar?"

"Just like that, only it's much smaller. Almost invisible. And pink. And with it, you can hear everything. Fairy mermaids can only do this after they find their one most special shell. They search and search til they find it. The one meant only for them."

"But where do they find their special shell?" she asks, looking worried. "What if they can't ever find their very own pearl shell?"

"They DO find the right one when they search everywhere under the sea. They always do this searching when they're exactly seven years old, like you. They look between the rocks and the coral and everywhere in all the sea gardens of all the oceans of all the world. They search everywhere, because each fairy mermaid has her own shell, the one meant ONLY for her. She can't just find any shell. It must be the exact one meant for her. She has to try out a lot of them before she finds the exact right one."

"Oh…" Daisy says, sighing with pleasure and smiling, her colouring forgotten. "How does a special shell work, when you can find it?"

Um, right. I wish I'd looked up hearing aids on my laptop or my phone before telling her this story, but now I need to sort of make things up. "It's a mystery that only fairy mermaids, like you, can know. I've heard they must search and search, but maybe they have helpers to find their shell, like computers and technology. I don't really know. Also, I think maybe the right shell has the power to find them. I'm pretty sure it's kind of tricky."

"But why?" she says. "Why don't people just give the

fairy mermaids the right shells? Or they could get them at the store."

"You're right!" I say. "I bet sometimes that happens. At the special mermaid shell store. When they first find the right shell and they put it up to their ear, sometimes it whispers and sometimes it whistles or makes nonsense sounds, like waves or the wind. Mermaids have to find the right shell and they have to try to listen really carefully for the right sounds. That's how the magic works."

She nods, still listening.

"You might find the right shell for some other fairy mermaid, but it won't work at all for you. And then when you do get the right one, it's hard to make it work at first. There's lots of different sounds all at once and you can't hear the fishes clearly. You have to, like, listen really hard to hear them."

Aunt Eira gasps. She tries to cover up with a fake cough.

Daisy stares at me in surprise. "Because there are little pops and air noises and all kinds of sounds and you have to listen AROUND all those other sounds to hear the fishes sing," I say. "And the whales and octopuses and, well, everybody else in the fairy mermaid kingdom are all singing and talking and laughing. All at the same time. So, you have to listen really carefully."

"I can do that," Daisy says. "I'm really good at that." That's one thing I like about my sister. She's fierce.

"I know you can," I say, getting up and going over to

give her a hug, even though I know she'll pull away. Aunt Eira has a tissue and is blowing her nose. I hope she's not getting a cold.

"Tell me more about the singing fishes," Daisy says, "Can you draw a picture of them for me? Please, Morley?"

Before I can say, "Sure!" we hear somebody at the front door and Danny clomps in, not even stopping to take off his boots. He's carrying what looks like a little red-faced doll with frowzy whisps of black hair in a baby carrier. Daisy leaps up and shrieks, "Daddy! Daddy's here! It's my Daddy!"

He laughs and puts the baby carrier on the table and grabs Daisy in a big hug and kiss. Then everybody has a good look at Lily and says what a pretty baby she is, even though she looks like a little old man with sunburn. They're hugging my mother and congratulating Danny, but then my mother says she's just so worn out. She needs a nap, she says.

Eira says she needs to talk to Danny, just for moment. Alone. They go to what used to be Danny's office and I hear the door close.

Gus gets Daisy to help him bring in more firewood while I help my mother up the stairs. Dom follows with Lily in her carrier. He says he's just running out to the car to get the carry bag of baby stuff and Mom's suitcase, while I turn back the bed and help my mother get her coat off.

She sits on the side of the bed and then just sort of sags down on the pillows, even though she's still dressed in a baggy old shirt of Danny's and her track pants. I pull off her boots, help her get her legs onto the bed and pull the covers up around her. Mom looks kind of grey, like she has the flu. I get her a glass of water and put it on the bedside table. I ask if she's hungry or if I can get her anything else, but she just waves me away. By the time I do all this, Dom has put the bags down next to the dresser and gone back downstairs.

Gently, I lift baby Lily out of her carrier, being careful to support her head and back with one hand and her bottom with the other, just like Aunt Sorcha showed me how to do. I lay Lily on her back in her crib. She doesn't have a coat on, just a fluffy yellow blanket, wrapped tightly around her, the way new babies like.

"There you go, little baby," I say. She fusses a bit as I unwrap her enough to check her diaper, another thing Aunt Sorcha showed me how to do. It's still dry. I wrap Lily up again and close the curtains. They're both asleep and Mom is starting to snore when I tiptoe out.

When I get back downstairs, all the adults are sitting at the kitchen table, drinking coffee. Daisy is bouncing around, talking about fairies and mermaids and the pink bicycle she got for Christmas because Santa came. Her Dad's finally here and she's all wound up.

Eira sends Daisy to our room to get her suitcase. I packed it for her already, but it wouldn't surprise me if she dumped everything out and just put in some of her toys and her bathing suit and Bunny Daisy, who she has to have or she can't sleep. I guess it doesn't really matter if that's all she takes to Danny's. She has clothes and books and probably everything she needs at her Dad's house. Or if she doesn't, he probably just goes out and buys more.

I imagine what that would be like, having a whole second set of everything with your other family. I haven't ever been to Danny's house, so I can't say what it's like. Daisy is useless at ever telling you something you want to know.

Someone knocks at the door and the baby starts to cry. "That's OK, I'll see about Lily," Danny says, surprising me. I wonder if he knows how to look after babies. But I guess he does. He probably learned when Daisy was little. "And I need to talk to your mom for a minute."

Eira comes back from the door, saying it was some people looking for a room for a few nights. "I had to say sorry, but no," Eira says. "With your mom just home, it's really too much. I sent them over to the Blomidon Inn." That's this old sea captain's house, just down Main Street as you head out of town.

I'm relieved. I look after the guest rooms all the time, cleaning them and changing the beds and making them all nice for the next people, but I don't want to have to do it all alone. Also, I'm learning how to do the breakfasts, but I don't want to have to do that alone, either. And it looks like right now my mother is too tired out from having Lily to get up and look after guests.

I had to stay in hospital after I got hurt last Fall, so I know what it's like there. It's always too cold, but they only give you these skimpy little blankets, thin as an envelope. They leave the lights on all night so it's hard to get to sleep, and it's noisy. If you ever actually do get to sleep, they wake you up to take your temperature or tell you they have to do some other test. The food is all terrible stuff you'd never eat at home. You need to come home just to get any rest. Or anything good to eat.

"Forgot to mention it," Gus is saying now. "Did you hear the Farmer's Market is closed?"

"From the storm?" Eira asks, pouring more coffee into each person's mug.

"Looks like," Gus says, wrapping his hands around the big mug he always chooses. "Big hole got tore in the roof, water poured in, then some pipes burst. Long and short of it, market'll be shut down for a week or two for repairs. Could be longer."

"Does that mean no Saturday market?" I ask, worried about how my mom is going to sell her baking. That's if she's well enough to do it, with me and Sheila, her usual baking helper.

Which reminds me, we should phone Sheila. Just to let her know. She's a teenager, but she's got a baby. I know she also has two part-time jobs. Helping mom bake is one of them.

"Well, Dom and I can check on any orders..." Eira says. "If there are any?"

They all look at me, as if I've got the answer, but I don't know. I get the baking order book from next to the landline and see that yes, there are some cakes and cookies promised. But, like Eira was saying, not very many. It's nothing like all the orders we had before Christmas.

Eira pulls out her phone, checks the number from the order book and calls Sheila. It turns out she knows about the orders, and she'll be coming over tomorrow to do the baking this week and then the deliveries. Seems that Mom already has it all set up. So that's one problem solved.

We're eating the stew when Aunt Sorcha arrives, saying something about she came as soon as she could get away. Aunt Eira gets up to get a bowl of stew for Sorcha, but she says never mind, she already had her supper. She goes to check on Mom and Lily. Not long after that, she's back downstairs saying Mom is a bit feverish, but she took some Aspirin and she'll be fine. And no, she says she isn't hungry. But when was the last time Lily had a bottle?

Aunt Eira looks embarrassed. Somehow, we forgot. We look in the pantry, find the bottles and the bottle cleaner machine and Sorcha tells me again how to put bottles together for Lily. She shows me how to store the bottles in the fridge and how to warm up a bottle and test it before giving it to Lily. She reminds me that babies need to not drink too fast and shows how to hold a baby on your shoulder and burp them. I feel like I'm in school, but I guess Sorcha would be a good teacher. There's no fooling around with her. It's just straight information. Do this, then this, then this, then you're done. Gus calls her a very no-nonsense type of person.

Sorcha checks that her number is next to the landline and in my phone, checks on Mom and Lily again and then she's gone. She'll be back tomorrow morning, she says. Or I can call, if I need her.

Just after that, Eira and Dom leave too, along with Pixel and all her cat toys. "Just a few more days before our big adventure, sweetie," Eira reminds me as they're leaving. "See you soon!"

Danny and Daisy go out somewhere, I guess to get some father-daughter time. I go find Gus in his workshop and help him make boxes for a while. Then I sit with Feather on my lap, purring himself to sleep while I read, until Lily cries and I go to see what she wants. I change her diaper and bring her downstairs, to let my mother sleep.

I put her in her carrier and warm a bottle, which she drinks while we sit together in the rocking chair. She's dry, she's been fed, I've been holding her, she burped a lot, but she's still crying. And crying. I don't know what else to do to get her to stop.

I'm starting to get a headache and walking around, sort of trying to dance a bit with Lily, which she seems to like, when Danny and Daisy get back.

"Here," he says. "Give her to me! Looks like you need a break." Gratefully, I hand her over. And, of course, she instantly stops crying when Danny sort of croons a little song to her. Something about Irish eyes and smiling. I wonder why I didn't think of that. But then, he's her father. I'm just her sister. No, just her half-sister. I wonder if Lily already knows this?

I've been expecting Daisy to be jealous of the new baby. After all, she's been Danny's only little girl til now. But no, she seems OK about it. She even wants to sit and hold Lily and have Danny take a phone picture of her, which he does. He also takes one of me with Lily and Daisy and sends a copy to my phone.

Danny says he's staying over in one of the guest rooms and that I shouldn't worry about Lily for tonight. If she cries, he says, he'll get up with her.

He and Daisy leave the next morning, right after the hot breakfast he makes for us. "Looks like it might snow again," he says. "We better get on the road." Daisy's already out in his car, waiting. Just like I thought, she did dump out her suitcase. I had to repack it last night, after she was asleep on her side of the bedroom we share.

Before they go, Danny puts his number in my new phone. He reminds me that anything Mom and Lily need, anything at all, any time, I can call him. Day or night.

I thank him to be polite, but honestly, he lives a whole hour away now, in Halifax. Too far away to be much help.

"What's all this about magic fishes that sing?" he texts a few hours later, which makes me smile while I'm thumbing in the answer.

three

DID YOU SEE THIS YET? Jayden texts, attaching a photo. It shows a real estate agent's signboard with She SOLD it! on a banner across the top. In the background, you can see the sign is in front of Sam's house.

What? I don't understand. Sam's house is sold? But where's she going to live when she gets back from New York City?

And why didn't she tell us she and her mum and Margaret are moving?

It doesn't make sense.

Jayden doesn't know, either. But he does send another photo, with another For Sale sign that also has SOLD plastered across it. This one's in front of our old school, Seabright Elementary.

Crazy. Who'd want to buy an old school? But I don't

have time to think about this. I don't care, all that much, to tell the truth. I DO care about Sam and especially about why something so big would happen and she wouldn't even tell me, her best friend. We tell each other everything. We always have, ever since third grade.

She didn't tell me, even though she was just here for a whole week. We had plenty of time together when we were talking and just hanging out.

So why would moving to another house be a secret? It couldn't be that she just forgot. You don't just forget something that big.

That's when I notice a text from Jayden. *Hey Morley did you know Sam's not coming back? Moving to Hawaii. Did she tell you?*

I text him back: WHAT? She's moving away? To Hawaii?

I text her: *You're LEAVING? And you didn't even TELL ME?*

She answers right away. *I'm so sorry. My mom says we have to. I just found out.*

Me: *You found out WHEN, exactly?*

Sam: *Today. On way to airport. Total surprise!*

Unbelievable. You don't just find out your home is sold already and you're moving and it's a total surprise. But why would she lie?

Me: *I can't believe you're my best friend and you didn't even tell me. J. says you didn't tell him either. Did you tell anyone? I'm so mad at you, I don't even know what to say.*

Her: Sorry. Couldn't help it...

Another lie. Me: *You must have guessed. Margaret must have told you.*

Her: I didn't want to tell you. I'm so sorry.

I'm so mad at her, I can't even answer. *Instead, I send a text to Aunt Eira: Did you know Sam is moving away?*

Aunt Eira: Yes. But only since yesterday. She couldn't tell you. Didn't want to ruin your Christmas. It was such a happy time together. Morley, I'm so sorry.

Me: You knew and you didn't TELL me?

Aunt Eira: It was Sam's news to tell. Not mine.

But I don't want an excuse for what Sam did. Or an apology. I'm so upset, I don't answer my aunt. I let Jayden know what I found out, which isn't much. Then I block Sam, my ex-best friend.

I pull out my laptop, which works, kind of, by running it through my phone like Dom, who's a genius with computers, showed me how to do. That's just until the service person shows up to connect the internet.

I check up on all the things we're going to do in New York City. I Google drive all around where our hotel is. And have another look at what our room is like. I look up all the beading and jewellery supply stores in New York and pick the three best ones to go to. And the art supply stores, where I want to look at getting an easel. That's what you put your work on, while you're drawing or painting it. So much easier than working flat, like on a table or my desk, the way I do now. Then I look at some YouTubes of the best fun things to do in New York.

I set up a countdown clock on my desktop with the exact days, hours, minutes and seconds until our plane lands in New York City. Which, right now, is 3 days, 18 hours, 22 minutes and 13 seconds. I watch it clicking the seconds down down down.

Waiting for that time to pass, but I can't just sit around and wait. I check on Lily. Give her a bottle, or rock her and sing to her, or change her diaper.

Just like I thought, Lily does mostly sleep, but only during the day. She cries a lot at night. I don't understand how all the crying doesn't wake my mother, but she's having no trouble sleeping, just about all the time. If Mom's awake, I ask if she'd like some tea, or a sandwich, or anything but she always says, "No, not right now."

I take her cups of chicken soup and sandwiches and apple slices with cheese, but mostly I just bring them back down to the kitchen again later, barely touched. My mother is looking more and more sick, but maybe that's just normal, after having a baby.

Aunt Eira says a lot of mothers like to eat less, after they have a baby, so they can get into their clothes again and not feel like they've got baby fat. She says if Mom isn't eating much, that must be why.

Aunt Sorcha comes over every evening and checks on her and Lily and says they're both doing fine.

I don't hear from Daisy, but I didn't expect to. She's

having fun with her dad and won't get back til about the same time I do, the day before school starts up again.

I do the laundry, fold everything and put it all away.

I change my mother's bed every day, while Aunt Sorcha is helping mum get a shower.

I try to think up some new ideas for fun things we can do at Pet Club at school.

I shovel the ashes out of the woodstove once it's totally cold and dump them outside, around the roses. Mom says roses just love ashes. I don't remember why, but it's something about minerals in the ashes feed the roots. I guess I could look it up online. I don't bother.

I vacuum the living room and dust everywhere.

I unload the dishwasher.

I gather up the garbage and sort the recycling and haul the bags and the bin out to the curb on garbage day.

I make more bracelets, for when the Saturday market re-opens and we need more to sell.

I don't have any pet portrait orders right now, so I draw pictures of Feather. And Pixel. And Tippy. That's Sam's dog. And Spirit, Jayden's horse. We can show them as examples of my work at our booth.

I help Sheila with the baking. Mom comes down to supervise but then decides we've got it under control and heads back upstairs. I do the kitchen clean-up. Sheila does all the deliveries.

I check that there's going to be enough to eat while I'm gone. We have a new case of milk formula for Lily. The pantry is full of cans of soup, beans, tomato sauce, pastas and rice. The freezer has meat, chicken, a lasagna, a couple of casseroles, frozen fruit and bread. The fridge has sliced meat and cheese for sandwiches, potatoes, carrots, apples and an already made-up salad. There's easily enough for Gus and Mom and Lily to eat while I'm away.

I check the supply of Feather's food and litter. Plenty of both.

I repack my bag and backpack and set them in the hall, with my coat and scarf on top. Soon, Sorcha will arrive with the twins to stay over and look after Mom and Lily while I'm gone. It's all set up.

Then, at last, it's the day we're going to leave. The countdown clock is at 0 days, 18 hours, 8 minutes and 2 seconds. Eira will be here any time now.

I look out the window *again*, wishing she'd finally pull into our driveway.

Outside, it's deserted. No one is walking by on Main Street. There aren't any cars passing. Not even any birds at the feeders. It just looks grayish and wet-cold, like a place you want to hurry through, not be in.

Overnight, most of the snow has melted. The snow-family Daisy insisted we all help her make on Christmas Day has turned into white lumps. The snow-mother is the only one that's still there, sort of. She leans over, her head almost melted away and her red scarf dragging on the ground.

Where is she? Why isn't she here yet?

"Morley, you know a watched pot never boils," Uncle Gus says, interrupting my worries. He's busy taking down Christmas decorations. "Cheer up! She'll be along soon enough."

I have no idea what pot he's talking about. Probably just another one of his old-timey sayings. I shrug and make myself come away from the window, turning back towards our living room. It looks nice, with the lamps turned on and a fire leaping about in the wood stove.

Yes, she'll be here soon. She will be. Just like she promised.

Gus reaches for the angel at the top of the tree. He's tall enough that he doesn't need the stepstool, like I would. I wish we could keep the tree a bit longer, like we usually do after Christmas. But even though I've been giving it more water every day, it's starting to dry out. What he doesn't say, but I know, is a dry tree is a fire hazard, something that scares us both. Time to get rid of it and put the house back the way it was before the holidays.

The tree is the last thing to go. When we're done, and it's just a dried-up evergreen, Gus and I carry it out back, leaning it against the wood pile ready to chop up for firewood.

Back inside, we sweep up all the fallen needles and that's it, we've un-Christmassed the house. Everything's gone til next year except the lights outside and the wreath on the front door.

Even though it's Holiday Season and winter in New York City, just like here, it will be so much better there. Who cares if it's snowy? Cities have so much to see and do. Way more than just read a book or make some bracelets or look after your sister or do your homework.

Or cuddle with Feather, which I'll miss while we're away.

And yes, we did get homework to do over Christmas vacation. How mean is that? I keep telling myself I should pull it out and at least look at it, but then I don't. And now, there isn't time. We'll be leaving soon.

We'll get to the airport this evening. Aunt Eira and I will lounge around, watching movies and eating snacks in our hotel room. Our flight is tomorrow morning, super early. We'll be in New York City – *New York City!* -- in time for lunch. I wonder where we'll be and what we'll be doing at *this exact hour, minute and second* tomorrow?

My stomach flutters, just thinking about it. About that exact moment when we're sitting in our seats on the plane and the pilot hits the accelerator and the engine roars and we're going faster and faster, racing down the runway. It's one of the most thrilling feelings, taking off in a plane.

Suddenly, you're looking out the window and buildings and trees and cars are getting smaller and smaller way down below. The ground vanishes because now you're in the clouds and then, flying above nothing but cloud pillows below. You look out and see clear sky and the tops of the clouds, and sometimes, other planes passing by. It's incredible!

I hope it's a clear day tomorrow so we can see all that.

My aunt still isn't here, so our Girls' Getaway still hasn't gotten started yet. I help Gus gather the Christmas decorations. We disconnect the generator and carry it back down to the basement. A generator is like a little engine. We used it to turn on the tree lights when the power was out. It was magic, to sit in the living room, all bundled up in blankets, with the little twinkly lights in the tree, a few candles flickering, and the generator softly humming.

I noticed that when there are no lights inside, and no streetlights, how bright the stars are.

It was the best Christmas ever. There was only one thing missing. I didn't hear from my father at Christmas, but then, I didn't really expect to. I've never met him. I don't know where he lives or what he looks like or hardly anything about him. Not even his last name. I hope wherever he is, he had a good Christmas. Though it probably wasn't as good as the one we had.

Gus hands me the angel. Daisy broke her when we were decorating the tree before Christmas. You can hardly see where Uncle Gus glued her back together. I wrap her in tissue and place her gently in the Christmas box, on top of all the other ornaments. He starts untangling the lights from the branches.

"So, all set?" he says. "Got everything you need?" He knows I do. Anything I forget to take, like toothpaste or enough pairs of socks, I can probably buy. He already gave me some money. "That's for spending, not saving," he says in his gravelly voice, "and don't go telling your mother I did that."

As if I would. One thing I've learned about money is that when someone wants to give you some, you take it and say, "Thank you." There's no need to tell anyone else about it, unless you're worried that they're only giving you money to do something you don't want to do. But that's not true now. There's zero chance of me telling my mother about a kind gift, or anything else.

Since she got home, she doesn't seem to be interested in talking to anyone. I only go in there to check on her and Lily. I don't stay long enough to give my mother a chance to say I can't go to New York with Aunt Eira.

I go over to look outside one more time. It's starting to get dark, which feels way too early. I step out on the front porch in my slippers, shivering, to get a better look for any taxis or ride-shares that might be coming our way.

But there aren't any. She's *still* not here. And now, the streetlights have blinked on. The moon has already risen and sits as if pinned to the sky, just above the park that's across the street from our house.

Lily cries then. I listen to hear if my mother is getting up to look after her. But no, Lily is still crying.

"Go ahead," Gus says. "Don't worry. Your aunt isn't going to leave without you."

I head upstairs, change Lily and she goes right back to

sleep, so I guess she isn't hungry yet. I'm just getting her settled again in her crib when I hear voices downstairs. That must be Aunt Eira, at last!

It isn't Aunt Eira at the door. It's Aunt Sorcha. Maybe she's already here to stay for the next few days so I can go away? But then why didn't she bring in her suitcase?

"Morley, did you look at your phone lately?" she says.

What an odd question. "Um, no. Why?"

"Well, you should do that now," Aunt Sorcha says, as Uncle Gus turns away, pretending to be busy closing up the Christmas decorations boxes.

Sorcha goes upstairs. I turn on my phone and find a text from Aunt Eira.

It's short.

So sorry, Morley, but have to postpone our trip. Something serious has come up. Will explain as soon as I can. Love you. Sorry.

That's all.

She's not coming.

We're not going to New York City.

She won't tell me why. Just that something happened. Something more important than our Girl's Getaway and being with me.

Something she doesn't want to tell me about now, but she will later.

But what can it be? And when will it be "later?" I don't

understand. Uncle Gus comes over and tries to hug me as I swipe tears away with the sleeve of my sweater. I push him away. I don't want hugs. I want my aunt to show up, so we can get going.

I look for another message from her, saying it was all a mistake. Or she's just a bit late, but she'll be here soon.

But there's no other message from her. Or anyone else.

Aunt Sorcha comes back downstairs, holding Lily.

"I'm so sorry, Morley," she says.

"You knew, didn't you?"

"She sent an email. I got it just as I was leaving. All it said is she can't be here to get you, that the trip is off, at least for now, because there was something she had to do. She didn't say what. Or why. Just that she'd explain when she gets back."

"Something more important than our trip?"

"I'm just telling you what she said. I don't know what that would be."

We're in the kitchen now. She thrusts Lily in my direction while she warms a bottle for her.

"When she gets back? Back from where?"

"I have no idea. I guess we'll both have to wait til she tells us more."

"When will that be?"

"I don't know, Morley. Like I said."

She takes Lily and the bottle. "Now, I'm going to go see if your mother wants to give the baby her bottle. I know you're disappointed, Morley, but I'm sure there's an important reason Eira had to cancel at the last minute. We'll just have to be patient to find out what it is." Aunt Sorcha's not a huggy sort of aunt, but she's not mean. At least, not on purpose.

After she's gone, I don't know what to do. I just sit there, in the kitchen, wishing I could be anywhere but here.

Anything could happen, Gus said. He probably meant any good thing. That's usually all he ever wants to talk about, is good things. Never bad things. Like how his house got burned down last Fall and he lost every single thing he owned. And his hands still hurt, because they got burnt, like my hands did when I broke into his garage to try to save him and Feather, who used to be his cat.

And how he used to be married, but his wife left him. Or she died. I don't know which one. He's never said, and I don't want to ask. But I do know they never had any kids. And he's lonely.

I think about my own bad things. All this past year, longer than that, Julia Maclean, the biggest bully at our school, was beating me up. I got hurt in that fire and when Daisy jumped out of a tree and landed on me which sounds funny, but it wasn't. It's why I had to go to hospital. Now, Aunt Eira has broken her promise to come get me. She's lied to me. The one person in our family I truly thought would never do a single thing to hurt me just has.

I've never felt so bad. Or so alone. Or so worn out from crying.

Anything can happen. Anything includes bad things.

Gus comes out to the kitchen. He puts a glass of cold water in front of me. And a new box of tissues. And a chocolate bar, but I'm getting a sick headache and don't want it.

He asks if I want to talk about it. I shake my head no. I say I just want to be alone right now. He pats me on the shoulder. He goes away.

Later, I check my phone again, but there isn't anything else from Aunt Eira. There's something from Jayden, but it can wait. There's another message from Sam, but I delete it. In my room, on my secret shelf that Daisy still hasn't found, I take out my Father Project book and try to write in it, or draw something, but just can't.

I pick up a book but can't get into the story.

I turn on TV, but there's nothing on.

I watch some cats doing silly things on YouTube.

I think about taking a bubble bath, but just don't have the energy to go do that.

Eventually, Aunt Sorcha comes downstairs again. "I know you must be terribly disappointed, Morley, but..." she says. "Can I get you something? Would you like a hot chocolate? Or maybe some ice cream?"

I just look at her.

"Well, I'm sure it will all look better in the morning."

I don't know how it could.

"I'll be back right after my shift tomorrow afternoon. Look after Lily. And your mother. Call if you need to."

And then, thankfully, she's gone. Gus went out to his workshop or maybe up to his room. The house is quiet. I'm alone. I check that the front door is locked. And the back door.

I lie in bed, wide awake, listening to the house make all its usual nighttime creaks and wheezes. It's ancient, built by my great-great-grandfather and his brothers after they came here from Ireland. I wonder if they ever really wanted something but didn't ever get it. I wish I could meet them and find out what happened, when this was their house.

I lie there, trying to get to sleep, even though that never works. I close my eyes and pretend I'm in my bed in our hotel room at the airport. Soon, we'll be getting up to go check in and then get on our plane.

I turn on my phone, looking for a message from Aunt Eira saying she's just late, she'll be here soon. There isn't any message like that.

What could be so important that she'd suddenly decided not to go on our Girl's Weekend and go somewhere else instead? Even though we bought all the tickets for the plane, and for going to see *Wicked*, and the hotel room is already paid for.

Nothing I can think of makes sense.

It just leaves this aching in my heart. Never in my life have I ever felt this bad, not even when I woke up in hospital after Daisy hurt me.

Or when Julia beat me up and told lies about me.

Or when Danny left our family.

Or when my mother thought I was telling lies, but I wasn't.

Then Lily cries. Feather is curled at the bottom of my bed, sound asleep like everyone else in our family. I'm still awake. Just let her cry, I think. She sounds as miserable as I feel. And what's wrong with my mother? Why can't she just get up and look after her?

Look after all of us. Like mothers are supposed to do.

Finally, I haul myself up, grab my robe, and go get the baby. Back downstairs, I warm a bottle for her and then we rock in the dark. Lily looks up at me and I look at the stars fading as the sun starts to come up. She dozes off between sips of milk, taking a long time to finish her bottle.

Feather tries to leap onto my lap, but there's no space for him. He wanders off.

My face aches from crying.

My head pounds from no sleep. But I guess I must have drifted off, because then it seems like someone is lifting Lily off my lap. I open my eyes to find it's morning. My mother is there, holding Lily with one arm. She says, "Come on, Morley, let's get you back to bed," but she doesn't say this in her usual mother voice. It's an angel voice, gentle like she never is, as she takes my hand and walks me down the hall, back to our bedroom. She puts Lily on Daisy's bed, then comes back to tuck me in.

Or maybe I just dreamt that happened. I don't know. But I wake up in my own bed. Daisy's bed is empty. I remember then that she's gone to stay with her father. Feather has left to, off to check on his food bowl probably. The smell of toast and bacon frying pulls me out of bed. I look at my phone. No messages.

We would have been at the airport by now. Just getting on the plane.

"Hey Morley-Mae," Gus says when I get to the kitchen. "How about bacon and eggs? I already took some up to your mother."

There's no sound from upstairs. No Lily crying. Nothing.

Just Uncle Gus and me. He munches on his toast. I taste the eggs, which aren't bad, a surprise. I didn't know Gus could cook. Another surprise is that I'm actually hungry.

Instead of feeling like crying, I'm starting to feel angry. At Aunt Eira. As well as still being angry at Sam.

"Seems to me you're having a glass-half-empty kind of day," Gus says that evening at dinner. It's just him and me, eating spaghetti. Mom did get up for a while, when Aunt Sorcha was here, but she's gone back to bed.

"What do you mean?"

He gestures at my milk. "Like that," he says. "Is your glass half full, or half empty?"

That sounds kind of dumb. Or maybe it's a trick question? But Uncle Gus isn't dumb, even though he's old. He doesn't tease, not usually. "I don't know," I say. "Maybe both? Aren't they the same thing?" Maybe this is a number question, like fractions and per cents. We have to learn that stuff in grade 6 math. I know that half of something is 50%. Half full or half empty. Same thing.

I've got half as many bracelets made up as we'll probably need for the next market day. We sold almost everything (nearly 100%) before Christmas. This means a 100% possibility of needing to do more bracelet work.

I've got half of my parents. 50 %. Just my mother.

We're half-way through Christmas vacation today. And we're half-way through the school year.

I used to be half of all the girls in our family because there was just Daisy and me. Now, I'm 33.33 % of the Star family girls. One of three, one-third.

"Nope," Gus says. He gets up, collects his plate and mug and turns to rinse them at the sink, then places them in the dishwasher. He's waiting for me to finish eating so he can do the same with my plate and glass. Or maybe he's waiting for me to drink the rest of the milk, so the glass will be 100% empty.

"Why not?" This seems silly, but I have to ask.

"It's the same amount of milk, true?"

"Um…yes?" I don't get where this is going.

"So that part's the same. But when you look at that

glass, do you see half full, or half empty?"

"It doesn't really matter if it's the same thing."

"Ah," he says, smiling. "Look closer, Morley. If you've got a glass of milk that's half full, that's a good thing, right?"

"Yeah. I guess. If you're thirsty."

"But half empty, not so good, true?"

I shrug. "I guess. Unless you hate milk." I don't see what that's got to do with anything.

"It's the same glass with the same milk. Or the same day you're having – half full or half empty. All depends on how you look at it."

"Yeah," I say. "Whatever."

"Your aunt let you down. You're disappointed. But sooner or later you're going to find out just what happened. You missed out on this vacation together, but she'll make it up to you. Another time. Meanwhile, today can be half full. Or half empty."

"Which one is it?"

"You tell me," he says. "It's your choice."

This makes zero sense to me, but I don't feel like arguing about it. A glass of milk. It's just silly.

"So, I have a blanket box to go deliver. Want to give me a hand with that?"

Sure, I think. Why not? It's not like I've got anything better to do.

four

Yeah, she didn't tell us. But so what? Got 2 b more she'll tell us...

I thumb in an answer to Jayden: *A whole lot more. So why the big secret? What else isn't the truth???*

You're angry. I can tell.

No kidding. I have every right to be. I can't ever remember arguing, I mean not just a dumb little squabble, but really getting angry and yelling at Sam. Not ever. I haven't ever been really angry at Jayden either. But now it seams they're both being jerks. I don't even know what to say to him. He just doesn't seem to get it.

Hey, gotta go. Catch ya latr.

Yeah, I think, whatever. There's no message from anyone else except Sam and I don't want to talk to her. No text or email from Aunt Eira. Another person I love – loved, thought I did – who's lied to me. AND broken a big promise.

AND is keeping secrets.

I wonder if Sam is at the beach right now, over there in Hawaii. Or if she's trying on one of the 25 new bathing suits she just went shopping for and her mum bought her, now she lives somewhere that you always need a different one. I bet you hardly even need any real clothes, if you live there. Just shorts and tees and sandals for any time you don't have your bathing suit on. Like it's July, all year long.

Why would you even think of back here, where the sky looks like it wants to snow again and it's cold? She spent all Christmas with me, with us at our house, and she laughed and smiled the whole time. She never even said what she was going to do, which was move away.

To Hawaii.

Forever.

Right after she was in New York City, where she gets to go to big shows and shopping in huge stores where they have anything you could possibly think of wanting. There're restaurants, way more than here, and you can see art. Real art. Sam gets to do all that. I'd love to go there and see it all, too. We were going to, Aunt Eira and I. We should be there now, doing all the fun things. But I'm stuck here in this dumb little town, with a bowl of popcorn and Gus, watching TV. Just waiting for the baby to wail again. And the days to go by til it's time to go back to stupid boring grade

6.

On the day before school starts, Daisy gets home. She's angry about her dad bringing her home. She wants to go live with him, but he explains he has to get back to work. He's a police officer – or that's what he says. I'm not sure I even believe him because he had to go to prison last year for stealing cars. Police officers don't steal things and go to jail. Well, sometimes they do on TV. Not in real life. I think he's a liar, too.

"IT'S NOT FAIR," Daisy screeches, red-faced and crying as Danny pulls away, looking grim-faced. I know how she feels, but I coax her back inside anyways and turn on Beat Bugs for her to watch with a snack.

Lily wails, maybe from all the Daisy noise, and I go to check on her. But this time my mother has gotten her and taken her back to bed. "Warm a bottle, would you Morley?" she says. I go do that.

Some days Mum gets up for a while, to supervise me and Sheila doing the baking, or just to sit in the rocking chair with Lily or read to Daisy. Sometimes she eats a little bit, then says she's too full already and look how big her stomach still is. Mostly she just seems sad. I know how that feels, too.

On the weekend, we had the make-up sleepover. The real one got cancelled because of the big storm. Only four girls could come this time. The rest were all away somewhere, or they just didn't answer back. We ate snacks and played games and watched movies and it was OK, I guess.

Aunt Sorcha came over and brought her two little boys, James and Peter. They're twins who are 3 years old. The girls at my party played with them and said aren't they just so cute until the boys dumped the chips and stomped them into the rug, screaming with laughter and Lily woke up and bawled. The party pretty much stopped while we cleaned up the mess and Sorcha put the boys to bed and I went and got Lily, who turned out to be a star. She just stared at all the girls, really surprised. My friends said she's so adorable, a baby doll. Which she is, when she isn't wailing.

I know Sorcha and Gus tried to make my sleepover party fun, but it just wasn't as fun as when Sam is there.

Eira texted, a couple of times. *We're in New York, Dom and I, because Sam ran into some difficulties here and asked for our help.*

What? They're in NEW YORK? Eira went there without me because something or other happened? Sam needed help for something? But she and her mother would be going to Hawaii by now, wouldn't they? Or they're already there?

So I text: *What??? I don't understand. Why isn't Sam with her mother? Why did you go there without me?*

Eira: *I'm not sure, exactly, about her mother. It's complicated. Will tell you when we get back. Sorry about missing our trip together.*

Me: *But why? I thought you were excited about our trip???*

Eira*: I was. Can't explain now. Talk soon.*

I text back a few times after that, but she doesn't answer.

I text Sam. No reply.

I look back over the texts she's sent me, ever since she left. It was just something about needing help. But she was with her mother and going to her lesson with Madame Boulanger and going shopping and to shows and all that fun stuff before they left for Hawaii.

So, I text Jayden, asking if he's heard from Sam about what's going on?

Nope. Just said she's OK and not to worry about her. Which I wasn't.

Me*: But it doesn't make any sense. What kind of trouble would she need my aunt to help her with? Why didn't her mother do whatever it is?*

Jayden*: Beats me. Guess we'll just have to wait to find out.*

I don't want to wait. I don't want to sit around, with nothing to do but think about all the good times we're not having together in New York. Or all the not-fun of pretty much everything here. I text him: *You don't do that to a real friend. Which I thought she was.*

Jayden: *Get a grip. It's like you want to be angry. Like you're really getting into being mad at her. That's pretty twisted.*

Yeah, I think, what do you know? Jayden lives on a farm, with his mum and dad and his favourite brother, Patrick. His other brother Elyot, who nobody likes because he's a bully and totally full of himself, is off playing hockey most of the time. Jayden hardly ever has to put up with him.

Instead, Jayden works with Patrick, who quit university a few months ago and moved back home to board, breed and train horses and sell them. He's been doing all that, and teaching riding, since he was our age. Now, Jayden works with him, just about every minute he isn't in school, which is easy for him anyways. Jayden never does any homework, but he always passes everything. He says working with horses is all he ever wants to do. As soon as he can leave school and work with Patrick all the time, that's what he plans to do.

It's like he knows exactly who he is and what he's meant to do. What his gift is. That's what Sam calls it. She says everyone has a gift to do something. Some people have more than one. If you're lucky, like Sam and Jayden, you already know what your gift is when you're a kid. Otherwise, you have to keep looking for it. Like me.

Jayden's lucky. He's brilliant with horses, like Patrick. He's got a great home and both his parents and no worries. He's got it all. Like Sam. Like Daisy. Like Liam at school. Like lots of people I know.

Just not like me.

five

Daisy is a total nightmare about going to school the next day. It's the first day back. I get it. I feel like being a total nightmare, too. But I can't, because I'm supposed to act like the big sister.

We both usually take the bus, but Uncle Gus says he'll give us a ride, seeing as how it's the first day. He moves Daisy's booster seat to his car. They drop me off first because middle school starts earlier than primary.

Sam isn't there. I barely see Jayden, just for a minute at his locker before third period. We don't have any classes together this term. We only have the same lunch period two days a week.

There's nobody to sit with at lunch. Or at least not my two best friends. We used to eat together every single day.

"Hey, Mors," Nicola calls over as I scan the room.

"Come sit with us." She's one of the girls who came to my sleepover. Sure, I think. Why not?

They're talking about Christmas. "So, what'd you get?" somebody asks.

This is code for I just want to brag about what I got. Other kids got trips to cool places and new sports equipment and their own TV in their room and stuff like that. Or like Jayden. He got an underwater camera, diving lessons and their family is going to the Virgin Islands over March Break so he can dive and take pictures every day. I make myself not even think about what Sam got.

I got a laptop and a phone, which is awesome. I just don't feel like talking about it. And I got Lily. Which a couple of the girls mention, like this: "Oh, lucky you. She's such a little sweetie!"

I guess.

I finish my grapes, shove the rest of my sandwich back in my backpack and say I need something from my locker. Then I head to the library.

We're not supposed to be there at lunch period, but I kind of sneak in and the librarian, Ms. Peters, is kind enough to pretend she doesn't see me.

I've read every single book there is about jewellery design and doing beadwork. I've read the entire three shelves there are about art and famous artists. I've also read nearly every book about dogs. And cats. Where I'm sitting is closest to the Nature and the Environment section. I pull a book out without even looking at what it is. I'll just sit here, on the floor, out of sight of everyone and just sort of pretend to read it until the bell goes off. My next class is history, which I like because it tells stories about people and how they lived, long ago.

Then I hear someone talking, which you're not supposed to do in the library. I sort of lean around the end of the bookcase to see who it is, because it doesn't sound like a kid. Or any of the teachers I know.

It's not.

It's a woman, or maybe a woman, but they might be a man. She? He? Them? It's hard to tell. They have hair that's longish on one side and almost shaved on the other. One side is green. The other is orange. All their clothes are like someone in the army, only totally black. They're not a grown-up, or old like our teachers. Also not a teenager, like from the high school part of our school. Our middle school is separate, kind of. We share the library, offices, two gyms and cafeteria with the high school people.

Next to this person is Marceline. Her family moved here last year from somewhere in Africa, I forget which country. She's in grade 8. It looks like they're working on something together. I kind of try to listen in, but I don't get it. Then I know why – they're working in French. My French isn't good enough to know everything they're saying. I just catch parts of sentences, here and there. I give up and put the book – turns out it's about climate change and how it causes fires, floods and other extreme weather – back on the shelf. Then the bell goes off.

Mr. Cadeau asks me to stay after, at the end of homeroom. When everyone else has left, he asks me about how I'm feeling about my classes and being back to school. After Christmas, he adds, which he hopes was happy for our family?

How are you supposed to answer that kind of question? "Um, yes. I mean OK. I guess. Pretty good."

It's a relief when he doesn't press for details. Instead, he says, "Some of your teachers are concerned about you not handing in homework. And falling behind. Especially Mr. Fafard. And Madame Donnelly."

That's math. And French.

"Mr. Fafard, particularly. He says he thinks you haven't grasped many of the concepts from grade 5 math and the result is you are in danger of failing grade 6 math. Unless something changes this term."

I nod. I've got more important things to think about.

"I know you had a problem with a bully last year. That can make people fearful. It is normal to be worried and cautious. To think you have to spend all your time protecting yourself after you've been bullied. When you do this, you can spend so much energy worrying about the bully that you don't do as well in your schoolwork. This is a very common thing that happens, with bullying. Could this be a problem for you, Morley?"

I look down. I don't want to talk about this. Don't want to be here. "Look, uh, I have to go. I need to be home when my sister gets home, because I have to watch her."

"Morley, you know, if you need help, we're here at school to see you are safe. And that you're successful in your studies." He hands me an envelope with my mother's name on the front. "Be sure your mother or father reads this," he says. "One of your parents must sign it. And please remember to return it tomorrow."

"OK," I say. "I understand. Can I go now?"

He sighs. "We'll talk about this again," he says.

Not if I can help it.

The house is full of baking smells when I get home. Daisy has cheered up a bit because Sheila made her a fairy mermaid cookie that she's eating while doing a dot-to-dot in an activity book and, at the same time, watching the Barbie mermaid movie. Also at home, no guests (good), Aunt Sorcha (bossy, but she doesn't stay long) and Feather (asking me to fill his dish). Uncle Gus isn't here, Lily and Mom are sleeping so I put a load of laundry in the machine, it starts grunting away and then I get some time to read. And try to think up some new ideas for Pet Club at school. And try not to think about Aunt Eira, or Sam, or even what the pet rescue shelter people are going to say when I see them tomorrow evening.

My mother gets up for a while and even sits with us for the dinner I make, cheese and onion omelettes and sausages. She still looks tired. She doesn't eat much.

It's almost time to turn out my light and listen to Daisy snore when I remember the note in my backpack. I slip out of bed and, using the light on my phone so Daisy doesn't wake up, I open the letter, don't bother reading it because I already know what it says and sign my mother's name – Aoife Star – at the bottom.

I'll give it back to Mr. Cadeau tomorrow. Just like I've done with all the others.

Right at the end of English class next day, while I'm trying to get out the door fast because it's the day Jayden has my same lunch period, Mr. Cadeau says, "Hang on a minute, Morley. There's someone I want you to meet."

I don't want to meet anyone. I'm hungry. And I want to ask Jayden something.

Instead, I'm following my teacher to the library. Ms. Peters just smiles at me, and says, "They're at the back, I think," which is where Mr. Cadeau heads to. And there, sitting at the same table where I saw them before, is the strange-looking person, wearing the exact same outfit, only now their hair is half green and half purple. Today, they look more like a girl than they did last time I saw them. Up close, they look older than a teenager. With the make-up they're wearing, it's hard to tell.

"Morley, this is my friend and our volunteer Murdo Delorme. Mo, Morley is one of my homeroom and English students. I thought you two might want to meet."

"Hey, Morley," the strange person says.

"Uh – hi, um..." I say, wondering how to get away. Mr. Cadeau has gone back to the front desk and is talking with Ms. Peters.

"Call me Mo," she (are they a she?) says, offering an elbow bump. "And my pronouns are they, them and their. So, what are you up to right now? Got time to chat for a minute?"

"I – uh – was just going to lunch," I say, which is pathetic, when I hear myself say it. I wonder if I should mention where the cafeteria is, in case she or he – no, *they* -- didn't eat yet. But no. I don't want to have to sit there and try to think up something – anything – to talk about.

"I know. Luc – I mean Mr. Cadeau – already told me. I like your necklace. When's your birthday?"

"What?"

"Your birthday. What month and what day?"

What an odd question. I'm not sure why I don't just excuse myself and go find Jayden in the caff, but the answer sort of pops out of my mouth before I think about it. "July. The 12th."

"So that's why you chose red? For the stones in the centre?"

I shrug. "Maybe. I guess so. Why?"

"Well, you're a Cancer."

This is getting stranger and stranger. "Cancer? I don't have cancer!"

"No, not the illness. The sign. For your horoscope. You're Cancer, the crab. And your birthstone is Ruby."

"Which is red," I say. "My favourite colour."

"Well, there you go then," Mo says, stuffing books and

papers into a beat-up looking leather tote bag. "Anyways, gotta go. But I'll be here tomorrow same time, if you want help with your math."

Fat chance, I think. But I get it, at last. Mo is one of the teacher assistants that help some kids out. The dumb ones.

"I don't think so. But thanks anyways," I say, just wanting to get away as fast as possible.

"Suit yourself," Mo says, but I'm already gone.

Jayden is nowhere in sight when I get to the caff. I don't see anyone else I want to sit with. Turning to leave, I'm cornered by Crystal and Tiffany. Two of my least favourite people. All last year, they were Julia's two bully-helpers. They apologized, sort of. But I think it's easy to just say, "Sorry," and that hardly means anything. It's just words.

They said Julia made them be mean, like her. Or, if they didn't do what she said, she'd beat them up. And tell lies about them on social. I think that's just an excuse.

Now Julia's gone, because she got sent to some special school to make her stop bullying, so Crystal and Tiffany are trying to be my friends. As if.

I tell them I don't want to hear what they've got to say and turn around, heading for my locker and then I don't know where, since it's not safe to hide out in the library anymore. It's got that Mo person, ready to use up our whole lunch time doing horrid math problems. Yuck!

I grab my books for afternoon classes and, in a bit of

luck, there's nobody at history class yet. I sneak my lunch out and gobble it fast so I won't get caught, and am sitting there with a book open when the other kids begin coming in.

Later, I think that Mo could be kind of interesting. Maybe I wouldn't mind talking to her, I mean them, if they didn't want to talk about math. I already knew about horoscopes, but hardly paid them any attention. Most of the time, I think what horoscopes say is just silly, like someone made it up. I'd never really heard about everyone has a birthstone, though. And mine is Ruby. That gives me an idea.

Secrets and Lies

six

Gus doesn't say much on the way to Sunflower Pet Rescue Shelter. I'm grateful. I've been thinking and thinking about what they might say. Sometimes at night when I can't sleep, I think about all the reasons they could say, "No." But then I try to remind myself of all the good reasons for them to say, "Yes."

Like Gus has already reminded me, it could go either way. And, either way, I've already done everything I could to present my best ideas to them, along with all the other help I've already given them. That help was being a volunteer with the cats and dogs, feeding them, cleaning out their cages and enclosures, walking the dogs and playing with them and cuddling the cats. I feel so sorry for them, that they just wait and wait for some kind person to come and adopt them. Like I adopted Feather.

So, me working there as a volunteer, and also giving

them money from making the jewellery and selling it at the market, led to the people that run the shelter asking me how they could find more kids like me who want to help the animals? I did a presentation with my best answers to this question. The presentation happened before Christmas. They said they'd tell me what they thought about my ideas at their January meeting. That meeting is tonight.

Here's what I suggested:

You could do pet camps for kids over Spring Break and another one during summer vacation. Kids would learn about dogs and cats. Maybe some of their families would decide to adopt a pet. And they'd pay money for the camp. That money could help the shelter buy pet food and supplies.

You could help kids start pet clubs at their schools.

You could start a Junior Volunteers program. Right now, you tell everyone they have to be 16 to be a volunteer with the animals, even though younger kids can do lots of things to help out, like I do. A lot of teenagers have school and part-time jobs, so they don't have as much time to volunteer as kids my age do.

Why not start Happy Paws groups? They'd be people of all ages, including kids and older people like grandparents and people with disabilities – just all kinds of people getting together to do projects for the shelter. One idea I had was maybe the Happy Paws could make friendship bracelets to sell at the farm market, because I always sell out on those and give all the money to Sunflower Pet Shelter. Happy Paws people would have a good time getting together and making new friends. Especially for people who live alone, it could give them something fun to do.

What if they say, "Yes" to all my suggestions? Will they want me to help doing all of them? Do I even have time, with school, and making jewellery, and art, and chores at home, and looking after my sisters? I don't know. Maybe.

What if they say, "No?" I guess I could just keep trying to talk them into it. Or take my ideas to a different pet shelter. Sunflower isn't the only one around here.

Or what if they can't even decide? It isn't one person who runs the shelter, it's a group of people, called the board of directors. They're all old, like Gus except for one guy, who's more like Dom, or maybe a little older. They said all kinds of nice things after my presentation, like you do to be polite. My mother was there too because she drove me. Mom said she thought the director people seemed very positive.

"No matter what they say, it doesn't change all you've done for them, Morley." Gus says now. "And they're grateful. And they made you their very first Junior Volunteer."

"The only one," I say as we get to where the meeting is, slip off boots and coats and sit down to wait to be invited in. We're the only ones waiting in the hallway.

"That could change. Because of you. Something to be really proud of, right there," he says. "You showed them it's possible."

"I guess."

Gus doesn't say dumb stuff like, "So, how's school going?" or "Were you pretty happy with your Christmas?" Or "Any word from your friend Sam? How's she liking living in Hawaii?" That's one of the things I really like about him. He's OK with just sitting there, not talking.

I'm sitting on my hands and thinking a thousand things, like what didn't I tell them about my ideas that I should have said? And should I have more ideas now, just in case they want to hear more? And …

Finally, Mrs. Piers-Smythe opens the meeting door and invites us in. She's the leader of the directors and she runs their meetings. There are just six adults there, sitting around a table. Each one reminds me of their name and says a brief hello.

Mrs. Piers-Smythe says, "Morley, on behalf of all of us and Sunflower Pet Rescue Society, let me thank you again for your volunteer work and for the generous donations from your jewellery-making business. We are really impressed with your contributions, and we all enjoyed your presentation last month."

OK, I think, that's good, but what about my ideas?

"So," she continues, "you'll be wondering what conclusions we have come to. Let me say first that we all saw the value in each and every one of your suggestions. Each of your ideas was well-thought-out and well-presented. Let's review these ideas."

I don't need to review. I know what they are. If they talked about them, all these directors must know what they are, too. I try not to look impatient. Or is Mrs. Piers-Smythe just dragging it all out because it's bad news?

"The vacation pet school to educate young pet owners, involving the community in donating their talents, supporting school groups, these are all very interesting ideas. We can see how they could be a fit with Sunflower's mission and goals, while appealing to young people such as yourself and the broader community..."

And there was some more like that, making me think that a big fat BUT was coming. And it was.

"... however, excellent as these ideas are, we feel that this may not be the appropriate time, given our current staffing and other resources. There are also concerns about how such projects could be managed, given the complexity of..."

Then there was something about, "these challenging times...limited time and resources...the every-increasing burden of unwanted animals...managing expectations...working with our community partners..."

By this point, I wasn't listening that closely because I could tell what was coming, just by looking around the table at all the faces. None of them was even looking at me. I did notice that one of them was doodling on a copy of the presentation I handed out to them last time we met. I wasn't close enough to see what it was she was drawing. Others were just sort of staring down at their hands, or off in space, waiting for Mrs. Piers-Smythe to finally run out of things to say.

"Do any of you have anything to add?" she said at

last. No one did.

"So, to get right to the bottom line and not waste anyone's time, what we have decided is that you, Morley, have demonstrated the value of having Junior Volunteers at the shelter. We will be starting the new Junior Volunteer program later this year and hope you will offer your thoughts on how it should operate. Perhaps you could tell your friends at school that we will begin accepting applications in March or April?

Some people around the table nod their heads, like they're in church.

I guess this means it's a NO to all my other ideas.

She repeats how happy they are to have me as a volunteer, and some of the people get up and come over to add their own thanks and shake my hand. Then, it seems, we're back out in the hallway, pulling on coats and boots.

"How about a milkshake at Scoops on the way home?" Gus suggests. "Or would you rather have pizza? Pizza Factory should still be open..."

"Milkshake, please," I say, not because I'm hungry, but I just don't feel like being back home yet.

To my relief, Gus doesn't go all, "Oh, poor you, Morley."

"You know," he says, slurping his milkshake just like I do, "they didn't say never. They said not right now."

"It's pretty much the same thing."

"Well, they did recognize what you do for them. With the volunteering. And giving them money."

I guess that's something.

"And you know, we don't need them to start the Happy Paws."

What? We don't?

"That one was a way to reach out and help others, not just the shelter. Shouldn't be that hard to do, either."

Really? I slurp, thinking.

He finishes his milkshake and rubs a paper napkin across his face, around where his mouth probably is, under all that mustache and beard.

"Sure. What do you need? A place to meet – well, that could be the library, couldn't it? Or the community centre? Or maybe one of the churches. Shouldn't be a problem finding some place that would work that we don't have to pay for, because it's an activity, open to everyone."

"Uh, yes. That's true," I say.

"And then, what else do you need? Put up some posters, get the word out..."

"Posters? Why wouldn't you just put it on social media? Text some people about it."

"Oh, right. You could do that as well," he says. "Get your Aunt Eira and Dom involved. They're good at that sort of thing, aren't they?"

Yeah, they are, but I don't want to ask them for any kind of help.

"Don't be sad or mad at those shelter people because they don't have your imagination, energy and vision,"

Gus says when we're back in the car, heading home with a take-out milkshake for Daisy and one for my mom, just in case she wants it.

"You have good ideas. Smart ideas. They just didn't see it. Yet. It wasn't a hard, 'No,' Morley. And everything that isn't an absolute, final NO is on a road trip to 'Yes!' "

"There might be some other reason they aren't even saying," I say. Some secret reason. Or they're just lying about wanting to listen to ideas and do something different. Or they don't even care what kids think.

"Exactly. No use wearing yourself out about it. Makes no matter. You still get to volunteer. And we can get the Happy Paws started. How about we talk about that after school tomorrow?"

We. Uncle Gus said, "We."

"Sure, OK. I mean thank you. That would be good."

I'm disappointed. I am. I'm trying not to think about how much fun those pet day camps would have been. I bet Daisy would've loved to go. Lily too. When she's older.

We already have a Pet Club at school, because I helped start it. But I bet they'd be a good thing to have at other schools, not just ours. Kids at the clubs could also find out about adopting pets and giving them a happy home. And about helping wild animals, the ones that are endangered, like the penguins and the sea turtles.

But at the shelter, at least kids will be able to

volunteer, if they want to. That's a good thing.

And doing the Happy Paws, with Gus. That'll be fun. I start thinking about what kinds of projects I could suggest they do. Like the friendships bracelets. Or wish bracelets, like I used to make and sell at the market. Of course, the Happy Paws will probably have their own good ideas, too.

Gus is the perfect person to talk about doing your craft and selling it. He makes beautiful jewellery boxes with real fossils inlaid in the tops, like the ones he gave Sam and Daisy and me for Christmas. When you meet him, you'd never think he's an artist. But when you see his boxes, you know right away that he is.

I wonder if Happy Paws could be a way for Gus and me to meet some more local people who are artists, or want to be, or that's who they truly are and they don't even know it yet?

seven

I tiptoe into my mother's bedroom to check on Lily. It looks like they're both sleeping. I take the mug with the tea in it gone cold and turn to leave, when my mother says, "Morley, wait a minute, would you?"

I clear a spot on the maple blanket box at the end of her bed – a gift from Gus – and sit.

"Your Aunt Eira just emailed. She said they'd be home late tonight. They'll come over tomorrow and bring dinner. And she mentioned something about a special surprise. For you. She didn't say anything else."

This is the most my mother has said to me at one time since before Christmas. Maybe she's starting to feel better. That would be good.

"She said she'd explain everything," my mother adds.

"Thanks for telling me," I say, though she's already

turned away. Wanting her privacy, I guess.

Back downstairs, I pull out my phone and see that Aunt Eira sent a text a couple of hours ago saying pretty much the same thing.

What do you mean? I text her.

Too complicated to tell you except in person. Getting back late tonight. Will be over like I told your mother, tomorrow. With a surprise for you. I think you're going to like it.

This just leaves me with more questions. And why doesn't she just phone and tell me? Why does it have to be a big secret til tomorrow?

I don't want a surprise. I want to know now.

When I try phoning her, it just goes to voicemail.

Maybe they went to the city about something to do with their wedding, so now there's some big news about that? I know Eira planned just a small wedding, really simple she said. She wants it to be here, in Seabright, not away. But she's told us that Dom's mother wants a big fat princess wedding in Boston with hundreds of guests and ice sculptures and an avenue of flowers, whatever that is, and a full sit-down dinner and live music from a band that's famous. Maybe straightening out her wedding plan is the reason we couldn't go on our Girl's Getaway?

I know she met Dom in New York when they were both going to school there, so could that be where their wedding is going to be? I guess they still have friends there and Dom's parents and some of his family live near there.

Or did they just go for some other reason? It couldn't be to buy Aunt Eira an engagement ring, because she already has the one she wants.

So why did Eira and Dom have to go to New York, instead of me and Eira going?

For some reason that meant a lot more to them than our Girls Getaway weekend. And I have to wait until tomorrow, a whole 24 hours from now, to get any answers.

Feather hops up on my lap and I gather him up for a cat hug. I bury my nose in his soft fur, smelling his sweet scent. Today, it's a mix of clean laundry and dust, with a hint of peppermint. Then I pet him while I whisper what I'm really thinking, the real things you can't say, even if you feel them. He's the only one I know who never, ever keeps any secrets and he never lies to me. Not ever. And he always listens. Maybe he's the only one I can really trust.

Next day, I'm munching through the cheese and pickle sandwich I made myself for lunch, not paying much attention to the conversation at our table. It's some kids from history class. They're OK, I guess. Not as much fun as eating with Sam and Jayden used to be. Better than eating alone and looking like a complete saddo.

Across the caff I spot the kids I wouldn't mind sitting with. One of them is Liam. Class President, popular, nice to everyone, super cute with floppy blond hair and eyes like milk chocolate. He looks up, smiles at me, and goes back to talking with the kids at his table.

Then someone says, "Dance" and I tune in to what kids at my table are talking about. Turns out it's the Valentine's Day Dance.

"But we might not even have one," Caitlin is saying. "After what happened last year. I guess a lot of parents were pretty mad about it."

What happened last year?

"Yeah, but that was some kids from another school, wasn't it?" Tara says.

Someone else explains, because her brother was in grade 8 last year and he was there. Some boys were outside, probably smoking or something, and these other kids just showed up. There was some shoving around or fighting. Someone called the police and everybody ran, but somebody else did a video with their phone, so there were kids that got in trouble. The administration said no more dances for the rest of the year.

Which seems pretty mean.

"So will there even be a Valentine's Day Dance this year?" Caitlin asks.

"I think we need to campaign for one, starting now," Sima says. "We might have to threaten a student strike if they cancel our dance."

Wow. But I can see where it would be totally unfair if they cancelled the dance, just because of some jerky kids last year.

Sima is still talking about telling everyone and getting organized and having to fight for what you want.

I'd rather think about just getting to go to that dance. With Liam.

Can he hear me thinking about him and how dreamy he is? There's a spooky thought! Anyways, just before the bell goes off, he stops at our table. Other kids are already leaving, when he says, "Hey Morley."

"Um, hey Liam," I say. How lame is that? My tongue sort of blows up and sticks inside my mouth any time he's around. I don't know what else to say.

"Got something to ask you," he says, with that smile. "See you at Pet Club?"

"Uh, yeah. Sure," I say, floating all the way to my next class, even though it's Evil Gym Class and we have to do basketball drills. The only thing worse is climbing the rope up to the rafters of the gym. Last time I tried, I was hardly off the floor when I got so dizzy I thought I couldn't breathe and I was going to throw up.

Unfortunately, you must climb the rope to the top to pass Grade 6 Gym, which in my opinion is a form of child abuse. I'm pretty sure I'm going to flunk gym class, even without the rope climbing. I don't really care.

It's hard to sleep that night. I mostly can't make my mind stop thinking about reasons why our Girl's Getaway didn't happen. I'm so tired the next day I just about fall asleep in English class. I really fight to keep my eyes open.

After school, I'm sitting in the rocking chair in the living room, giving Lily a bottle, when someone knocks on the door. I call for Daisy or Gus to answer it, but no one's around. Guess they're out in the workshop.

I grab the throw off the couch, wrap it around and over Lily, and go answer the door. I hope it isn't more people looking for a room for tonight. Even though I put a note on the door saying that, unfortunately, we're closed until February.

It isn't some people who want to be guests. It's Mr. Cadeau. He looks as surprised to see me as I am to see him. But we can't stand here, letting the cold come in, so I ask him to step into the hall. "Thank you, Morley. Actually, I'm looking for your parents."

Right. "Well, Mom's asleep right now. She just had Lily, you know," I say, pulling the throw off her.

"Ah, she's adorable. How fortunate, getting a new little sister," he says, putting down his briefcase and reaching for her. "How about if I hold her while you go get your mum."

"I don't think she can…" I say.

"Just ask her please, Morley," he says in such a kind voice that Lily actually smiles up at him! But then, she's a total flirt with men like Dom or her dad or, looks like, Mr. Cadeau.

I leave him sitting on the couch with Lily watching him adoringly.

To my surprise, Mom is coming down the stairs. She's wrapped one of her ratty old robes around her, over pajamas. She has bedhead. "Who's that I heard you talking to?" she says.

"Mr. Cadeau. My English and homeroom teacher."

She gives me that what-did-you-do-now look. I turn and she follows me into the living room.

"Mr. Cadeau," she says. "I see you've already met Lily."

"She's a darling, Ms. Star," he says. "Congratulations."

They go on like this for a few minutes – how was your Christmas? How long were you without power? We haven't had much snow, not since the big storm. The kind of stuff adults say. By now, Mr. Cadeau has handed Lily back to Mom, who hands her to me. "Morley, maybe you'd take Lily back up to her crib? And I think she might need a change?"

I get the hint. They want to talk. Probably about me. Zero points for guessing what about. Once I get Lily settled, I eavesdrop anyways. Even though I know it's wrong to listen in on conversations.

It sounds like Mr. Cadeau has brought all those letters he sent home and I signed. There's silence for a few minutes. I imagine her glancing through them.

"No," she says. "I didn't see these. It seems my daughter has signed them, to save me the trouble of doing it myself while I was pregnant. And recovering."

"Yes, I think you're right," my teacher says. "But I think we need to move forward with helping her, with geometry and also her marks in gym. Some parents might dismiss it, but a pass or better is required in both subjects to move on next year to Grade 7."

"Yes," my mother says. "Well, I'll speak to her about trying harder."

"As her teacher, I don't think the problem is not trying. She does turn in acceptable work in English class. I've talked to some of her other teachers and they tell me she's a good student, overall. The problem isn't because she doesn't try, I don't think."

"What else could it possibly be?"

"Not all students learn all topics in the same way, at the same speed," he says. "In math, I think Morley might have missed basic concepts taught earlier and then after that less and less of what was taught makes sense to her. So, she falls behind. It would be natural for a bright child, or any intelligent person, to try to cover that up. There can be...well, embarrassment. Confusion. Anger, even, that they aren't understanding. Nothing to do with how smart you are."

"I see," my mother says. "Well, to tell you the truth, geometry wasn't one of my own best marks in school. And gym class, that was a joke. I never saw the point of it, to tell you the truth. The things I enjoyed, like dancing and hiking and skating, weren't ever offered in gym class."

"Exactly my point. The same could well be true for Morley. We all can't be excellent in every subject. As I said, she does well in most of her classes, English and History particularly. Math and gym aren't her favourites. But we can help her not have a miserable time in her classes while learning the basics so she can be successful."

"What are you suggesting?"

"Tutoring, for one thing. And helping her build her confidence in her abilities, in all subjects, including the ones more challenging for her."

Tutoring. Yuck. I don't want to have to sit with some boring old person like last year when I broke my wrist and couldn't write my tests.

"Tutoring?" my mother says. "I'm afraid that's just not possible right now. I'm out on mat leave, and…"

"There would be no cost," Mr. Cadeau says. "I have a…well, a colleague, at school, who is able to tutor some students in math and French."

"Morley has her responsibilities at home. I need her home right after school…"

"Which she will be. Tutoring is during the school day. At school."

"With a teacher?"

"With Mo, a teacher's helper who is directly overseen. By me."

I don't hear what they say next, but then they're in the hallway and it sounds like Mr. Cadeau is leaving.

It seems like it's all decided, even though no one asked me. I wasn't even allowed to be in the room.

I go to see to Lily a bit later, expecting there to be a big scene with my mother about school and the letters and why can't I do better and all that, but Mom's in the shower, so I change the sheets on her bed and then scoop Lily up and bring her downstairs. I figure it's better for her to be with us, not just parked in her crib all the time. She still cries a lot, especially after she has a bottle. When she's not crying, she's OK. I guess.

Next day at lunch I was thinking how great it would be to go hang out in the library, but then I remember I have to go see the tutor. I don't see any way of getting out of it. What was her -- I mean their -- name? Jo? Flo? No - Mo. I'm already late.

They should be happy I'm even there. They probably get fired or something if their students just don't show up. I know this is mean thinking, but so what? It's what I think.

"Hey, Morley," Mo says when I take the seat across from her, with my lunch hidden on my lap so I can sneak bites. "Glad you could make it. Go ahead and eat your lunch. Ms. Peters says that's OK."

I just nod yes because my mouth is full of cold pizza, left over from yesterday's supper.

"So, tell me what you hope to get out of our time together?"

This is so funny I just about choke. Getting out of it is exactly what I want.

"I know. You wonder why you're here? From what I hear, it's to catch up with your friends in Grade 6 math, right?"

"I don't care if I catch up. Who really needs to know that stuff?"

"What stuff, exactly?"

"Well, how to figure out ratios. Or fractions. You can just get your computer to give you the answer."

"I see. So, you think it's fine to rely on a machine to do your thinking for you? Some of it?"

"Yeah," I say, offering Mo one of my cookies and biting into the other. "If I ever need that stuff, which I won't. Or maybe I'll just get a robot to do it."

"You're sure about that?" she asks, taking a sip of coffee with a bite of cookie. "But how can you know what you're going to need to understand for the whole rest of your life?"

I shrug. "I'll just Google it."

She smiles. "Well, that might work, if you're always going to be near a computer? If you know what the right question to ask is? If you already have a pretty good grasp of math basics to understand how it works."

"I guess," I say. "You don't need to know any math to be an artist."

"Well, even artists need to frame their work, or go do their banking and take care of their money, or pay their taxes, or – all sorts of things. Every day. It all requires some basic math."

I don't say anything, just sneak a look at the wall clock, wishing the bell would go off so I could escape.

"OK, maybe we can agree to not agree about math being a really valuable skill when you grow up. Let's talk about now. What do you want now?"

To not be here.

To live in a world that doesn't have any fractions, or figuring out measurements, or things on graphs and charts, or ANY kind of math.

To have it magically be a year ago, when I could go eat lunch with Jayden and Sam every single day. And my mother wasn't sick. And life was just – normal. Mostly.

To live somewhere more exciting, like a city.

To have more pets and fewer sisters. And never do homework.

"Well, one thing you might want is to pass Grade 6, right?"

"I guess."

"And what if math wasn't so hard? What if it was even kind of fun? Like a game? What if you never had to worry about passing math tests?"

As if that could ever happen.

"OK, let's talk about something else. What do you like to do, when you're not at school? Sports, maybe?"

Ugh. No.

"Music? Do you play piano? Or another instrument?"

No.

"Like to go hiking, or swimming, or maybe canoeing?"

"I like to swim," I say. "In summer."

Mo sighs. "I like your bracelets. That red and orange one is really unusual," she says.

"Thanks. It's one of the new designs for my Aunt Eira's store. On Etsy."

"I see. Well, wasn't that lovely of her to get it for you?"

"She didn't. I made it. I make jewellery to sell. Also art." I don't know why I need to tell Mo this. It just sort of slipped out. In case they're thinking I'm just another dumb kid who doesn't know anything.

Then Mo wants to know all about what kind of art I do, and is there some place they could see it, and there are more questions. The kind of questions the shoppers at the Saturday market ask sometimes.

"OK, Morley," Mo says when the bell rings. "Here's the deal. I can teach you enough math to pass Grade 6 and Mr. Fafard won't always be on your case about it. You teach me how to draw like that," and they point to a couple of doodles in the margins of my notebook.

I consider. "I thought we have to spend all the time on math?"

"We do. I'll come over to your house after school, two days a week, for art lessons. And we'll meet every day, here, for math lessons. During lunch or your free periods. Here's your schedule Mr. Cadeau made up for you. What do you say?"

I've never even thought of teaching anybody how to do art, except for Daisy and she doesn't count.

"Sure," I say, and we do a fist bump. "We can try that. See ya!"

Later, I'm sort of dancing around with Lily, when she

suddenly gives me a big smile. My Aunt Sorcha says babies don't smile because they're happy. It's just them passing gas. I prefer to not believe her. My aunt, that is.

As we dance near the bay window in the living room, I see Aunt Eira's red truck pull into our driveway. She gets out of the driver's side, and someone else gets out of the other side. They're not tall enough to be Dom, so who could it be?

As they get closer, I can see clearly who it is.

Sam.

But how? Why? Isn't she supposed to be in Hawaii with her mother? Or was that a lie, too?

I go to call Mom to let her know they're here, change Lily since we're upstairs anyways, and when we all come back down, Aunt Eira is in the kitchen, wrapping foil around a big casserole dish before sliding it into the oven. Gus is there, but once Mom, Lily and I get to the kitchen, he's got an urgent box-making situation out in his workshop and escapes.

Daisy is sort of bouncing around, wanting to know if Aunt Eira brought her anything from the city, and can she have some cookies, and why is Sam here?

Good question. Mom sends me to put a movie on for Daisy. She says she needs to talk to Eira for a minute.

I get Daisy set up with her movie and the new pink headphones Gus bought her so she can watch movies as loud as she wants and no one else (like me) will be annoyed. Sam watches me, not saying anything.

"Morley, I'm sorry..." she says, as Mom and Aunt Eira come into the living room with mugs of tea for them and glasses of milk for us plus a plate of cookies and tarts.

"Morley, I'm so sorry I had to cancel our trip together," Eira says, drawing her feet up under her and settling with a cushion on one end of the couch. Mom's in the rocking chair. Sam sits in the window seat. I sit on the piano bench.

I don't know what to say to this. They might think what I'm going to say is, "Oh, never mind, it's OK." It so isn't.

Or I could say, "I was so disappointed." As if they didn't already know.

Or: "You really let me down." That's pretty obvious, isn't it?

I shrug.

"And I'm sorry, too. Really sorry," Sam says. "I know how you must have felt..."

That's when I lose it. "Do you? Really? You know how I must have felt when we had all of Christmas together when you KNEW you were moving away forever and didn't say one SINGLE word about it to me? Or to Jayden? Your two best friends. Or used-to-be friends?"

"Um, well, I couldn't..." Sam says.

"It's not what you think..." Eira says at the same time.

"Really? It's not that you thought you'd just sneak away, and we wouldn't even notice? We wouldn't even mind that you were gone without telling anyone?" I hear myself shouting this. Lily, alarmed, is starting to fuss.

"And you," I say to my aunt. "We planned the Girls' Getaway for, like, months. You KNEW how special it is to me, about all the things we were going to do together, and then you just, didn't want to go or something?"

"It isn't like that," Eira says. "Let me explain…"

"Explain what? You found something more interesting to do? It was more fun to go to the city with Dom than with me? So that's what you did, and you couldn't even let me know?"

"Well, we were just so busy," Eira says. "There was so much to organize, and so little time. And Sam was in real trouble…our tickets and lawyers and, uh, other things…"

"Lawyers? What? Did she somehow get arrested or something?" even while I'm saying it, the whole idea is crazy.

"No, nothing like that. She was – uh, lost, but fortunately kept her head and reached out for help and we went down to see that she got home safely…"

But that can't be true, either. Her house is sold. Her mother went off to Hawaii. And I know her Dad lives in California. "Her home? Where is that, exactly? The one that's here is sold. Oh yeah, that's another thing you sort of forgot to mention over Christmas, isn't it?"

Sam looks ashamed. "I'm so sorry, Morley. I just couldn't…"

"Couldn't what? Tell the truth? I'm beginning to think that everything you say, our whole friendship, is just one big LIE!" Lily starts to cry. Even Daisy pulls off her headphones and says, "Be quiet, Morley! You're ruining my movie!"

"You're right, Morley. Sam's mother did sell their home. She has moved, to Hawaii. That's where she is now."

"But Sam isn't."

"No. Obviously."

"No," I say. "Why?"

"Well, she got, uh, lost..." Aunt Eira says, shooting a look at Sam that says *Here's the story and we're sticking to it.*

Sam doesn't say anything.

I guess that's possible. In a big city. But wouldn't you just pull out your phone and meet up again?

"At the airport," Eira says. "Ms. Park was already on the plane. And Sam, well, Sam wasn't."

"You somehow just forgot to get on the plane?"

"I didn't forget. I just ...didn't." Sam says. "I couldn't."

After all the times Sam HAS gotten on a plane, to go to music camp and competitions and off to see her father and to stay at Madame Belanger's in France all last summer – Sam couldn't get on a plane? I simply don't believe it.

"You missed your plane somehow and you didn't just, like, take the next plane to Hawaii?"

"Uh, no. I didn't" Sam says.

"Why not?"

"That doesn't matter now. Sam's here, back home and safe. She'll be staying with me and Dom."

She will? Why? This isn't making any sense to me. "Just til you leave again?" I ask Sam, who's looking ashamed, which in my opinion she should be. I'm sure she's lying. I don't know why and, right now, I don't even care.

"So, you should know, Morley, that Margaret is coming back. We don't have room for everyone at our condo – you know it's just got two bedrooms – so for the time being Margaret will be a guest here and also help your mum out with Lily. Just til we buy our new house and then Margaret will be with us." Eira says. "Maybe Sam would help your mother go check the dinner and set the table while you and I go upstairs and decide on which room Margaret would like? And I'll help you make it up?"

Is this some kind of dig, like our rooms are left messed up after the last guest and I didn't even get them ready, even though we've got the bed-and-breakfast closed right now? "No, thank you, Aunt Eira," I say in my coldest, most formal voice. "ALL our rooms are perfectly made up right now. YOU don't have to do anything. You've been SO helpful already."

Normally, I would never talk to anybody like this, but I'm so angry, I feel like the top of my head might explode.

"An apology is just empty words to you, isn't it? So

don't even try to pretend you're sorry. You left, you lied about it, you didn't get on the plane with your mother for some reason, then you tell this big story about being lost. You lied. You just left and threw away being friends with me and didn't even care. You ruined my special vacation with my aunt. That I looked forward to ALL YEAR!"

Sam looks shocked. She doesn't say anything.

"Morley, that's not fair," Eira says.

"I hate you both," I say. "I don't even trust you anymore, about ANYTHING. Don't even try any more phony stories. It's all just a big fat pack of lies!"

I'm keeping it together, at least long enough to get out of the room. It would be humiliating for them to see me cry. I go to what used to be the playroom but now it's the room I share with Daisy. I gather up my pillow and duvet and some of my books and art supplies. I take everything up to what used to be my bedroom, the one that's now rented out to guests but it's MINE, and I slam the door. And lock it. Then I throw myself down on my bed, in MY room, and ugly cry.

Later, much later, after they've tried to knock on my door and tell me to come down for dinner and I ignored them, I rinse my face with cool water and take some headache tablets. I have a shower and wish I'd brought up my pajamas, but I can get them later, after the whole house is asleep.

I pull out my phone, delete all the messages from Sam and from Eira, and block them both. I unfriend them on social. I delete emails.

I pull out my art supplies. Try to draw, but it just looks like scribbling.

Eira knocks at my door. "Go away," I say. "I'm not interested in anything you have to say!"

She sits down on the floor outside my door and says it anyways.

"Morley, you're totally wrong. About everything. It wasn't Sam's fault."

I'm not listening.

"She got separated from her mother, in the airport. Then she couldn't get on the plane. It left without her."

I look around for my earbuds. I want music. Not this!

"She tried to make her way home. But got lost and...the police found her."

So what? "She still could've gotten on the next plane," I say, not bothering to hide the hard edge in my voice.

"She couldn't get the next plane. Her mother was...arrested by then."

Oh sure. This whole story is getting dumber and dumber, like a bad movie. Even worse than the kind of movies Sam's father makes that are all about explosions and somebody chasing you with a helicopter and stuff like that.

"There was no one to help her. Her mother was in trouble, on the plane and then in Hawaii. Her father is making a movie somewhere in Asia. She asked me and Dom to help her."

Of course she did. Just in time to ruin our vacation.

"You were home, warm and safe with your family. She was all alone, in a huge city she doesn't know, abandoned by her mother and afraid. She had no one to turn to, Morley. No one to help her. No one. You are surrounded by family and friends..."

Yeah, right. Ex-friends.

I open the door. "I'm still mad," I say. "She – you – ruined everything."

"I know you're upset," she says, trying to hug me. I back away, crossing my arms in front of me.

"I'm not upset. I'm angry. Really, really ANGRY. At her. At you." Then, suddenly, I see it all clearly. "You went to New York City. The same place you and I were going to. I just bet you stayed at the hotel WE were going to stay at, didn't you? And you probably also went to see *Wicked* with HER, too?"

I can see in my aunt's face that I'm right. "Well, we had the reservations. And we weren't going to waste the tickets..." she says.

"You just gave our whole time together away. And then you lied and lied..."

"I can't believe you'd be so heartless, Morley. That you wouldn't even care that your best friend was alone. In danger. And scared."

"Which would never have happened if she'd gotten on the plane with her mother. But she didn't. Whose fault was that?"

"You don't understand," Eira says. "And it's not about

blame."

"I'm not a baby, like Lily, who doesn't know much of anything yet. And I'm not stupid, either." Even though Mr. Cadeau and some of my other teachers think I am.

She interrupts. "No one is saying you are a baby. Or not smart, which you are."

"Here's what I understand. You promised this special time together. We made all the arrangements. I helped pay for it, my part, out of my jewellery money. I was really, really looking forward to time together and all the fun things we'd do."

"I was, too," she says and manages to sound a bit sad, but I'm not fooled.

"...but then you went without me and didn't tell me why. I was left just waiting and waiting for you. Then, after days of you not even telling me anything, there's this crazy story about Sam not going to Hawaii but getting lost or something, which doesn't make any sense. So THEN, you did all the fun city things with Sam and Dom, not with me."

Eira just sighs. "I'm sorry you feel that way. It wasn't like that. Why won't you listen?"

Right. So now she's blaming ME, which just makes me even angrier. "So, here's the part I don't understand. I don't understand a friend who LIED to me, someone who was my best friend ever since grade 3, so that's a long time. Now I wonder if she even was a friend? Ever? Or was she just lying and faking everything? And I don't understand my aunt, who used to be my favourite aunt, who also lied to me."

"Morley, you're making this into a whole huge drama when really, it was just a change of plans. You know Dom and I are going skiing in a week, Sam too. We could add you if you want to go – to make up for not going to New York City?"

Skiing? Like in the mountains? How can you go to a play, or see all the beading and jewellery supply and art supply stores, or go and look at art at some ski hill? Probably all you'd see is snow. Is this some sort of joke? "No," I say. "I don't want to go."

"Well, OK. Suit yourself. I just thought you might want to get away, with Margaret here to help out. And it would be a good chance for you and Sam to make up. I'll leave you now. Maybe you'll be, uh, feeling better about things tomorrow. When you've had a chance to think it through."

"No," I say, "I know what happened."

"Well, sweetheart, good-night then. We can talk some more about this later. You know I love you. Always have. Always will."

She tries to hug me again. I turn away, ignoring her. I hear the door click as she leaves.

What I'm feeling isn't just anger. Or that I got cheated out of something. Or lied to, over and over. And they're STILL lying, because what they've said just doesn't make sense. No one just 'forgets' to get on a plane. And then gets lost. And THEN doesn't call her parents or anyone in her family or even their housekeeper, Margaret, but calls their friend's aunt, who they hardly even know. It's all lies.

I'm worn out from crying. And fighting. And feeling lost. And scared. And alone.

Most of all, what I'm feeling is betrayed. By the two people I thought would never hurt me.

Someone leaves a tray outside my door. Later, much later, when I'm sure the whole house is asleep, I take the tray back down to the kitchen. I scrape the food into the garbage and leave the dish to soak in the sink.

Then I make a strawberry chocolate smoothie and drink it, sitting at the table.

I gather up clothes and books and take them upstairs, to my bedroom. Mine again. If there's any guests, which there aren't, tough, they can sleep somewhere else. So can Margaret. I'm tired of having to share with Daisy.

I'm also tired of always being nice. Always helping out. Always doing what everyone else wants. Or needs. Or expects.

It's time to stop hoping that other people will do the right thing, say the right thing, tell the truth. Share. Be kind.

Because they won't and they aren't.

It's time for me to do all those things for me. To look after myself. And not ever, ever let them hurt me again.

Sitting at my desk in my room, my real room, in the dark, looking out at the stars and thinking and thinking because I can't sleep even though I'm so tired, the thought comes into my head: all the people who are supposed to love me but don't aren't the only ones who know how to lie.

eight

eight

Everybody's talking about the dance. I imagine what it would be like to go. There weren't any dances in primary, so this will be the first one ever for our class. I imagine Liam asking me. What he'd say. What I'd say back. It wouldn't be at Pet Club. I think he'd be cool and wait. Maybe come up to my locker. Or phone, after school. Or text?

No, he wouldn't just text. He'd get to one of the classes we share, science maybe, or history. We'd be the only ones there yet. He'd say, "Hey, Morley. I was thinking, do you want to go to the Valentine's Dance with me?"

Or, no, this would be better: "How about we go to the dance together?"

Or even, "I'd like it if you'd be my date for the dance? Say yes!"

And I'd say something like, "Liam, I'd love to go to the Valentine's Day dance with you."

He'd come to pick me up. His Dad would be driving. Or maybe his mom. I answer the door – no. Gus does. And then I come down the stairs, while they're both looking up at me. My hair is in an up-style, and I have real make-up on, not just lip gloss. Heels? Maybe. What sort of dress? Red? No, blue is better. Summer sky blue. With a halter neck and a gathered skirt. I'd make earrings and maybe a bracelet to match.

I'm coming down the stairs and Liam looks up at me with THAT smile and then he says, "You look really nice, Morley."

And I'd say, "You look really nice, too," because he's wearing a suit and tie and handing me a flower corsage. He looks so totally dreamy my knees kind of melt.

And Gus says, "Hey you two, have a great time," as Liam opens the door for me, and then …

Then I realize we're at school, Jayden has been saying something or other to me and I notice other people are starting to get here for Pet Club.

"Uh, sorry," I say.

"Never mind. Tell you later," he says.

Then everybody is there, and we get started.

We talk about different things we could do this term. Liam talks about finally getting the pet he really wanted, a bearded dragon. Jayden tells about his new dog-sitting business. I tell the others about what you get to do when you volunteer at Sunflower Pet Shelter. How they need more junior volunteers. I hand out copies of the volunteer application form. A couple of people seem interested.

Jayden says they have three rescue horses and a rescue donkey at their farm. "We're always happy to have barn helpers," he says.

We talk about what kids can do to help animals in need.

Then we talk about what we'll do next meeting. When people are leaving I kind of dawdle til it's just me and Liam. Now, I think. Ask me now. "Hey, good meeting," he says. "I like how you always try to get everybody talking. And that's interesting, about the volunteering for pet shelters. Anyways, I've got to get going. See ya!"

It's not that he's shy about asking. Maybe we just haven't hung out enough yet. Maybe he doesn't even know that I'd like to go to the dance with him. That could be it. Then I get this great idea. He said he just got a pet bearded dragon. That's an interesting pet I don't know anything about. BUT, I have a YouTube channel about pets where I talk about cats and dogs, so I'm a petsfluencer. It has advertising on it to raise money for Sunflower.

Here's the big idea. What if we do some YouTubes about lizard pets? Like me talking to him, at his house. It would be great.

That's what happens. I go to his house, we record enough for a whole bunch of videos about bearded dragons and it's cool. We have a really good time together. We talk and laugh a lot, but he doesn't ask me to the dance.

Or, at least, he isn't the one who does. It's Jayden who says, "Hey, want to go to the dance with me?"

I hesitate.

We're standing at his locker. It's getting awkward. He says something about you must be glad Sam's home and I was sort of sorry to have to give Tippy back to her, he's such a fun dog.

Say something, I tell myself. Do I want to go to the dance with my best friend? Uh, no, that would be so weird, slow dancing with your best friend. But I can't say it, at least not like that. I have to kind of fudge it and say something like I'm not sure. I'll have to ask my mother.

"Got it," he says, looking disappointed. "Find out and tell me tomorrow. Or text me later."

So that leaves me thinking I could tell him I'm already going with someone else, then just hope Liam hurries up and asks me.

But he doesn't.

I guess I could ask him. But I don't. What if he says, "No?" That would be so embarrassing.

A few days later, one of the girls who came to my sleepover texts to say *Hey did you see this? Tiff is going steady AND he gave her this cool bracelet and it's not even her birthday!*

I click the link to Tiffany's Snapchat and feel sick. It's got Sending You Sunshine stickies all over it. There she is, with her arms around a boy like she's an octopus, and you can clearly see the bracelet. It's one

I made. He must have bought it at the Saturday market. Probably when I was taking a break because if I'd sold him something, or even if I just saw him there, I'd remember.

Over on Tiff's Insta, it says *Goin' to the V-DAY Dance!* There are more pictures of the two of them.

Her new boyfriend is Liam.

Yeah, I know people break up all the time. They might not even still be together, by the day of the dance. But still.

Then it seems that everybody's talking about who's going with who and what they're going to wear (girls) or that it's just dumb and they're not even going (some of the boys) or they're trying to not talk about it at all (me).

I tell Jayden I've decided not to go. He looks hurt but doesn't say anything. After that, he kind of avoids me. Which I barely notice, because I've heard Sam is back at school and I'm always on the look-out to avoid her. We don't have any classes together, so it turns out not to be that hard, though this one time, I did see her in the hall between classes, coming towards me. I ducked around a corner and down a stairway, along that hall and up another stairway, which was the longest way to get to my next class and I was almost late, but it worked.

Gus and I put together a poster about the first meeting of the Happy Paws. We do it on my laptop, but we don't have a printer. He says, "Just send it to Eira. Or Dom. I'm sure they won't mind running up a few copies for us."

I don't want to ask my aunt for printing. Or anything else. Gus thinks I'm just being stubborn. But then, it turns out I don't have to ask my aunt, because Gus does have a printer.

And there's another surprise. The "ideal location" he mentioned for the first meeting turns out to be our old school, Seabright Elementary.

"But how could we meet there? Somebody bought it," I say. "Though who'd want an old school?"

He's grinning. "Well, you never know," he says. "Could be somebody who just LOVES going to school."

So clearly, not me. Sam, maybe. School is ridiculously easy for her, another totally annoying thing about her. Or Jayden, who always passes, even though he never studies or does any homework.

"You know who bought our old school, don't you?" I can tell he's just dying to tell me.

"Well, I'll give you three guesses."

I groan. That sounds like the kind of dumb game you'd play with Daisy.

"Maybe the town of Seabright bought it, like for offices or something?"

"Nope."

"OK. Then the county. Same reason?"

"Still nope."

"I don't know. I give up. Who is it?" Not that I care all that much but might as well humour him.

"Me. I bought it."

WHAT? "Why would you do that? I mean, what for?"

"For homes. There's more folks who need affordable homes around here than there's homes for them. Or apartments. I figure the old school is right in town, close to everything. It's got trees and plenty of parking. It's a good solid building. Town Council wants more housing, so they're willing to be reasonable."

"You're turning our school into apartments? Or condos?"

"That's the idea."

"But where will you live?" I knew Gus would be leaving us, when he bought another house with his insurance money from the fire destroying his old house. Maybe if he used all his money for the school, he'd stay with our family? I'd like that.

"One of the units at Seabright Garden Homes. That's what I'm calling it."

Oh.

"Anyways, I got the keys to the place today, so I'm celebrating. It's mine, officially. The school people left some tables and chairs and other stuff behind, even a printer. Have to get Dom to show me how to use it, I guess."

"I could show you," I say. I'd seen my mother using that printer lots of times, back when she was our school's secretary.

So that's what we do. Next day, he puts all the posters up "around town." This means on the notice boards at the post office, the Independent Grocery Store, the library and at his church.

It seems just so strange to be back in our old school. It's cold and kind of dusty, as if nobody's been there for ages and ages, even though I went there for years, all the way from kindergarten to the end of grade five. That seems so long ago. Now, it feels kind of creepy to be there.

"I'll turn up the heat some before the meeting," Gus says. "I think they left a coffee-maker in the teacher's lounge. Maybe better if we meet in there, come to think of it."

It's hard to even imagine this place will turn into people's homes. Gus shows me a diagram of the school and what it looks like, turned into apartments. He shows me where there will be bigger homes, with three bedrooms, or a bit smaller, with two. There will also be a couple of studio apartments, he says. He's delighted about what a beautiful old school it is. It's such a shame to leave a place like this standing empty, he says. He talks about how much he's looking forward to it, as a project. "You can help," he says. "Your sister too, if she wants to."

Somehow, I can't picture Daisy being much help. I'm also worried about my mother getting enough guests for our bed-and-breakfast, with one less guest when Gus moves out. Before tourist season starts up, about the only guests that come to town are parents of the university students, here for a visit. Or for graduation, in April. And with the Saturday market closed and a lot fewer bakery orders at this time of year, how will we have enough money?

Gus is still talking about where the shared gardens will be and how it's only three blocks from the harbour and how much families are going to enjoy living here. I guess he's right, even though it's hard to imagine this place being anything but a dusty old school.

There's a huge uproar at our new school the next week. The administration – that's the principal, mostly – has announced that there isn't going to be a Valentine's Day Dance this year. Instead, before then, there's going to be a Father-Daughter Dance.

By later the same day, some kids are picketing, right on the edge of the school property. One of those kids is Jayden. GENDER BIAS his sign says. Other signs say: UNFAIR! And DON'T TAKE AWAY OUR DANCE! Then everybody is talking about how come only girls and their fathers get to go to the dance?

Some girls, I think. The ones that have fathers. That leaves me out. Sam, too if her father is still in Asia or somewhere, making a movie.

The administration caves and makes it a Parent-or-Guardian-and-Student dance and announces that anyone that feels that he, she or they are being excluded for any reason should come to the office to discuss it. As if anyone will do that.

Jayden says he's cool with it. His mum is his date, he says. She thinks it's funny. He says Dom already said he'd take Sam. I guess I better come up with a plan to be doing something really fun, or at least look like I am, on that night so I don't look like a saddo who isn't going to the dance.

Every day, there's a lunch-time lesson with Mo and I

eat my sandwich while I have to learn math. I look after Lily, tell stories to Daisy, help Sylvia with the baking because we're starting to get more orders, plus there's homework and all the usual chores to do at home.

Mo is making the math lessons at least better than Mr. Fafard ever does. Mo is also way more patient about explaining things. They promised they'd try to make it fun and, sometimes it almost is.

It's way better on the days Mo comes over to learn drawing. Mom was nice about saying it's OK.

Mo says the thing they'd really like to learn how to draw is their motorcycle.

"You've got a motorcycle?" Wow, I think. How cool is that?

"Yep. My spons...uh, uncle helped me buy this wreck of a bike. It was at the back of some old guy's shed. All in pieces, mostly in old cardboard boxes. Luc helped me put it back together."

Mr. Cadeau did that?

"So, would you maybe take me for a ride? Some day?"

Mo grins. "Tell you what. Get a C in math and get your mum's permission and, sure, we can go for a ride. This summer."

Some days my mother gets up, at least for a few hours. A couple of people call about getting me to do portraits of their pets, I guess because they saw the one I did of Jayden's horse, Spirit, that's hung up in the waiting room of his mum's vet clinic.

I make bracelets, go to school, hang out some with Gus, don't hang out at all with Jayden or Sam, and do more bracelets because the market is opening again.

Mo and I, and sometimes Daisy, do drawing together. And eat cookies, while Lily watches from her baby seat. She's totally fascinated by Mo.

Aunt Eira comes and goes, but I don't want to talk to her.

Gus and I get ready for maybe five or ten people to come to the first meeting of Happy Paws. We're completely surprised when so many people show up that we don't have enough chairs for everyone. We explain about the whole idea behind Happy Paws is to get together, make some things to sell to raise money for pet shelters and meet new people. I tell them that I'm going to show them how to make simple bracelets to sell at the market. I say it's fun and pretty easy. I tell them all the tools and materials will be supplied.

It doesn't cost money to join the Happy Paws groups. We pass around a sign-up sheet and talk about ideas of things to make. And tell them what it's like to sell things at Saturday market, how it's fun to chat to the people and pretty easy to do.

At the next meeting, I demonstrate making three types of friendship bracelets. Some people are good at doing bracelets and pick it up right away. Others aren't as fast at learning how, and a few say it's too hard, but they'd like to make something else, if that's OK?

Of course it is, we tell them.

Some people talk about other crafts they can do, like crocheting and embroidery and making bird houses. A couple of people want to knit. Someone else does beaded slippers and wants to show how to do them. It seems like they're having a good time. The only disappointment, for me, is that they're all grown-ups and mostly old people. None of them are kids.

With making pet YouTubes, getting tools and supplies for the Happy Paws to make jewellery and figuring out what to show them how to do next, school and Mo and everything else, I don't give much thought to the dance.

Then one night, at dinner, it's just me and Gus. Daisy has already gone to do something or other and Mom didn't come down. "So, I know you don't want to talk about this, but…"

ARRGH. When adults say this, it always means we are going to talk about it.

I hope it's not about why I'm pretty much avoiding Jayden and totally avoiding Sam. And Aunt Eira. Even though they keep trying to talk to me.

"How about we go to the dance, you and me?"

It's the last thing I'm expecting. I don't know what to say.

"I know I'm not your dad. Not trying to be. Just that, well, I messed up on my Grade 6 dance. That's some time ago. Thought maybe you, being a good person, might want to give me another chance."

OK, I think. Put like that, how can I refuse? I'll go.

I need a dress. With mum sick, and Aunt Eira -- well we know about why that won't work -- and Aunt Sorcha never wears anything except her nurse outfit or jeans, she's hopeless at dressing up. Who can I ask to help me get the right dress?

"What do you say, Morley-Mae? Is it Morley-Maybe or Morley-yes?" Gus says and I realize I still haven't answered him.

"Sure," I say. "I mean yes. I'll go with you. Thank you for asking me." We already learned in health and relationships class that you thank someone for inviting you to a dance. And you thank them for dancing with you.

"It'll be all right, Morley," Gus says. "Trust me on this." And, surprisingly enough, he's right.

Mostly.

Secrets and Lies

nine

I get home from school one day to two surprises.

Usually, I'm not really a fan of surprises. In my opinion, surprises are usually bad. Especially at my house. I'd rather have some idea of what to expect most of the time. It just makes everything easier.

SURPRISE ONE: a post card, dropped on the table near the door. I take a minute to look at the picture. It's a city street with a lot of yellow taxis and a big plume of steam puffing out the top of an orange striped pipe in the sidewalk. On the back, it says "A shopping district street in New York City."

The postcard is addressed to me, in black pen. The message is from Sam. Strange to get it now, more than two weeks after she got back to Seabright.

It doesn't say much, just thanks again for all the fun we had at Christmas, and I loved being with you and your family.

I loved our Christmas together too, but now it seems so long ago. Like it happened to some other Morley, with some other Sam at some other Christmas.

There are voices coming from the kitchen. One is familiar. It's Sheila. The other voice, a woman's, has an accent. Spanish, I think. This woman sounds a lot like Margaret, who used to be the housekeeper at Sam's house. But it can't be Margaret, because I heard she went to work for another family.

SURPRIZE TWO: It IS Margaret. She's baking cookies with Sheila. Gus is sitting at the table, joking about his job as a cookie tester and how hard he has to work.

Margaret? Here? Then I kind of remember someone saying Margaret would be coming to stay and help us, whatever that means. Looks like she's helping with the cookie orders right now.

"Ah, Morley, it's good to see you," Margaret says. "Your sister is in bedroom, playing, your mother and baby are fine, upstairs, lie down. Nothing to worry about. Why don't you sit down? Have snack? Tell me, how is your day?"

Uh...right. All I want to do is grab something to eat and escape to my room. Good to know everyone is OK and I don't have to rush upstairs and see if Lily needs something. Or Mom does. Or worry about Daisy.

"Margaret...uh...hi," I say. Margaret is a good person. She's always been kind to me like she is to all Sam's friends. "Did you, uh, did you find..."

"My room? Yes. Gus show me." I hope he didn't give

her MY room. He looks at me and winks. I try to smile, even though I'm not happy about Margaret being here. Even if she does make us dinner and do laundry and all those other jobs at home, she's Sam's Margaret. More like Sam's mother than her real mother ever was, at least whenever I was around.

She's in the Sam camp, not in the Morley plus Daisy plus Lily plus their mother camp.

I remind myself that Margaret is just here because she needs a place to stay.

That she'll only be here til Aunt Eira and the future Uncle Dom buy a big house where they all can live. Including Sam. And Tippy. That's Sam's dog. Not someplace I ever intend to visit.

"Well, you think about," Margaret says now, wiping a hand across her forehead and pushing black hair out of her eyes. The kitchen is hot and she's a rather wide woman who's only a little taller than me.

Later, I come back down to see about something for dinner. Sylvia has gone home. Gus has also gone off, probably to his workshop. Or maybe to his new-old school project.

Instead of an empty kitchen and having to look in the fridge to see what I can make for us, Margaret is there. And so are the wonderful smells of something cooking for dinner.

"Morley, hamburgers and chips for dinner in ten minutes," Margaret says. "Maybe you call Daisy? And also see if Señora your mother is hungry? Then, after we eat, we bring Lily down for a while?"

It's later, after dinner, after we clean up the kitchen, when I'm giving Lily a bottle, that I ask Margaret why she's here.

"To help Star family," she says simply.

"I mean, I thought you left looking after Sam because you got this other job?"

She looks surprised. "Señora Park ask me to leave. Say she moving, to Hawaii. Sam also. Job is no more. Say she hear Señora Bailey-Smythe needs housekeeper.

"Then Señora Bailey-Smythe, she wants me to come back from Mexico fast. *Ahora!* Right now. I don't want to do this, but I do. I work for her, but things not so good there. Then your Aunt Eira, she ask me to come here, help your mother. Help you. Do that and stay here. Also, in afternoons, get Sam from school. Help them. But sleep here. Soon, they move out of little condo and get new house. Big house. Then I live there."

I think about this. It's true, we need the help. Margaret needs a place to live and a job. "Is this what you want, too?"

"I help where I can. Your mother. You. New baby. And down in Mexico, even with my family, my kids, so happy to be there, but always when I am there, I miss Sam."

Yeah. Me too. I miss the old Sam. The one who was really my friend.

Margaret is here because she needs a place to stay until there's room for her at Aunt Eira and Dom's house, which is also now Sam's house.

She says I don't need to worry. About the baby. About my mother. About making the meals and looking after Daisy and Lily and – well – everything.

She says I've had to do too much, maybe worry too much, for a kid.

She says she will do all she can to make things easier for me. Better for all of us.

I mutter, "Thank you, Margaret," and head off to my room. The upstairs one, with the window that looks out at the sky and off towards the ocean. The one that's always been mine, til we got renters. And then guests.

My mind seems to be zinging around, but my body feels like it's made of stones. I sit at my desk thinking this is crazy. I don't have time to do nothing. I need to go see how mum is. Check on Lily. See what crazy Daisy is up to. Make my lunch and hers for school tomorrow. Check my backpack, I think there's some English homework to do and a chapter to read in Science. And Mo asked me to just try to do five decimals problems before tomorrow. Just five.

Put out Daisy's school clothes for tomorrow. And mine. Which reminds me, the laundry basket is full again.

I probably need to clean Feather's litter box. And when was the last time I cleaned the downstairs bathroom? I should go do that. And isn't tomorrow garbage day again? If so, the recycling has to be sorted. It and the bin have to go out to the curb.

The market is opening up again on Saturday. Do I

have enough bracelets and other jewellery to sell? Are we all organized, for selling the cookies? I should check.

Are there any orders for jewellery I've missed? Or pet portraits? I don't think so, but I need to look at that, too.

But I just sit there. It's like I can't even move.

Like I'm frozen.

Finally, I pull out my Father Project book and start to draw.

I look at the math problems on the bus the next morning. They seem to sort of ooze around on the page. I can't make out what you're supposed to do with them. I give up and do my English homework, which is writing three paragraphs about my favourite book (it's *Alice in Wonderland*). By then, the bus is pulling up in front of our new school.

I used to be able to ride my bike or walk to our old school, but the bus to our new one takes 45 minutes. So now I have to get up earlier for grade 6.

The one good thing is Sam is never on our bus. Margaret always drives her. Or Dom now, in the mornings. Jayden takes a bus, too, but he gets up even earlier than I do to look after their horses before school.

I quit Pet Club, saying I have just too much going on, which isn't the actual reason. It's just easier not to see Liam there all the time and work with him on club plans. And wish that stupid Tiffany would disappear or at least quit Pet Club. She doesn't even like pets.

I cut back volunteering at Sunflower to just one time a week, usually Sunday afternoons, even though I still like the pets there.

I plan some more jewellery projects for Happy Paws and buy extra tools and lots more beads and cord for them to work with, along with jewellery wire and findings. That's earring backs and all the other little metal pieces you need to make jewellery.

I write an email to Sam about all the reasons I'm mad at her. Then I hit the delete button.

I do the same with an email to Jayden.

I'm still too mad at Aunt Eira to write to her.

I take out my plan for the bride's crown. It's a surprise for Aunt Eira, for her wedding this summer. It will be the largest, most complicated piece of jewellery I've ever made. I shove the half-made-mess of a crown, and all the fancy crystals and seed pearls and gold wire for it – the whole awful thing, into a box and push the box to the back of the top shelf in my closet. At least I don't have to look at it.

I pull out The Father Project again and write him a letter. Another one. Can't send it, because I don't know where he is. Maybe he'll want to read my letters to him, after I find him.

I help Gus some afternoons after school, over at Sea Garden. That's what we've started calling his school-turning-into-homes project. It's just shorter and easier to say than his idea for a name.

"Is Sea Garden the fishes' garden?" Daisy says, one day while we're eating the lobster lasagna Margaret left for us. It's just Gus, Daisy and me. Mom didn't want to come down. "In the ocean? Where they sing?"

"I'd like to be. Under the sea. In an octopuses' garden. In the shade," Gus sings, and she giggles.

It's just Uncle Gus, Daisy and me most days for dinner. Margaret makes breakfast every day for us, and packs lunches for Daisy and me, and leaves us a hot dinner. She cleans and does the shopping and helps with the cookie baking. On school days, we hardly see her. But I have to admit, she makes really good dinners for us. And there's a lot I don't have to do, like the vacuuming and laundry, now she's staying with us.

So yes, I'm grateful. But also wary. What if she's just reporting back to Eira and Dom about what goes on at our house? About how my mother still doesn't want to come out of her room or get dressed? About how she hasn't gone outside even one time, since she came home with Lily and that was weeks ago?

One day, there's a note from Eira. Not an email, an actual card, with a kitten on the front. I don't really want to know what it says, but then I get curious, so I open it.

If it's about you-should-be-nicer-to-Sam or another one of her I'm-sorry messages, I'll just stop reading.

But it's not. It's just – Morley, we need to talk about the jewellery you make for our Etsy store. There are some orders (details below) and also have you been thinking about new designs? ~Love always, Eira

Right. To tell the truth, I've been trying not to think of

any of that. But when we started our jewellery business, the online one, I was excited. We talked about it, about what if there's no orders? Or what if we get busy, with lots of orders? And what kind of customer service we want to give people. That's promising that they get what they ordered and don't have to wait and wait for it.

I did that. I made those promises. I look at the list and get started. It takes me all that week, staying up late, and just about all weekend, to make all the orders. It seems people want some of the new horoscope ones, especially the ones with red beads or crystals and a little silver heart instead of the horoscope charm, for Valentine's Day presents.

I get it all done. Each day, just about, Margaret is taking jewellery back to Aunt Eira, and bringing notes back to me about OK, this is good, please do this or that next.

There's no one else to do it for me. No way to get out of doing it because, after all, it's what I wanted. What I agreed to. What I promised to do.

So, I do. Even though, somehow, it's just not as much fun as it used to be.

And the strange thing is, each time I hand Margaret another package of necklaces, bracelets and earrings, each one in its own little satin bag ready for Aunt Eira to send to the customer, I feel happy about getting it done.

Each time I look in my bank account online because Dom showed me how to do this and see money coming in from the jewellery that sells online, I feel happy, like I accomplished something special. Some people, somewhere, who I'll probably never meet, are going to be happy to get this jewellery for a gift.

One day, an In-Service day at school so I'm home, Margaret and I are in the kitchen. I'm eating breakfast. She sits down with a cup of coffee.

"I'm thinking what we do to help your mother," she says.

"Don't know," I say. Aren't we already doing everything while she does hardly anything?

"I think, maybe, she has depression," Margaret says.

"From having a baby?"

"Many women have this problem, after a baby. Very tired after being pregnant and then the baby is born." She sips her coffee, looking at me as if expecting something. I don't know what she wants me to say.

I guess I can see how being pregnant would make you tired. But Mom has been in bed for weeks now, hardly ever getting up, even to look after Lily. She hasn't done anything at all for Daze or me.

"So, I don't know, I'm not doctor. But she need some kind of help. More than you do and I do. And your sisters, and aunties, and Señor Gus. More than we can do." She waits while this thought sort of sits in the air between us.

"You mean like maybe she's sick? Or she might need medicine or something?"

"Maybe. We can't know unless she see doctor. So I tell this to your aunties."

And there it is. Right there. Margaret IS here to spy on us. I shove back my chair. I don't want to talk to her at all. Anything I say might get back to anybody.

"You need to know, Morley, there is family meeting today. Here. To find what we must do," Margaret says as I'm rinsing my dishes to put in the dishwasher.

A family meeting. I'd rather eat fire ants than go to one of our family meetings. They're always about stuff nobody wants to talk about. Like bullying. We had that one last year about me getting beat up all the time by Julia. Or there was one when Danny left. People shout. Or they cry. Or they stomp out of the room. These family meetings are awful.

I put on my headphones, turn up my music, and get into the latest bunch of jewellery orders. When they're all done, I have a look at my homework, and do some of it. Then I spend the rest of the day reading.

After I hear Margaret leave, I head downstairs for snacks.

I check on Lily a few times. Change her. Feed her. Burp her. Rock her. Dance with her. Sing to her, because she likes it.

When I get just sick of being in my room all the time, I get Lily into her bunny snowsuit and me in my coat and boots and tuck her into her stroller. We go for a walk, along Main Street, around the park and back. The sun is out and it's almost like an autumn day, with the snow all melted, except the trees are their skeleton selves, snoozing through winter.

By the time we get back, Lily's asleep. Her cheeks are

rosy.

It's time she gets out in the world a bit, I decide. We both should.

Aunt Eira is the first to arrive. I look to see if Dom or Sam is coming in behind her, but no. "Morley, sweetheart, how are you doing?" she says, handing me her coat and scarf to hang up while she peels off her boots.

What are my choices? Circle the best answer:

    A. Really good. Having a blast. Couldn't be better.

    B. Good enough.

    C. The truth.

    D. Don't ask.

I don't answer, but she doesn't seem to notice, because Aunt Sorcha comes in next, with her two little boys. Daisy squeals to the boys and the three of them run to what's now her room. Daisy LOVES playing with James and Peter which is fortunate because, to tell the truth, I don't.

Sorcha goes to "see that they're settled," which, translated from Mother-talk, means, "see that Daisy doesn't have finger-paint or glitter glue or some other dangerous materials out where two three-year-old little monsters could redecorate with them."

Meanwhile, Mom comes down, looking like she just woke up and needs a shower. She's in pajamas and mule slippers, with an old shawl sort of thrown around her.

Margaret brings in a plate of cookies and little cakes and lemon bars. She asks what people want to drink. I follow her to the kitchen to help carry the drinks.

My mother looks confused, sitting on the rocking chair but not rocking, her tea ignored. Somehow, she seems smaller than she used to be, like she's shrinking.

Aunt Sorcha, on the couch, looks determined. Between bites of cookie, she says she can only stay for half an hour. She's got a late shift tonight and, she says, she's hardly seen Chris for the past week, he's working so many double-shifts. He's her husband and our uncle, but we hardly ever see him.

Aunt Eira is at the other end of the couch. She asks Margaret to stay, but Margaret excuses herself, saying she'll be up in her room, if we need her.

I'm wishing Lily would cry, so I could get out of here. And, just like Lily can hear me making that wish, she lets out a squawk that could frighten a whole colony of cats. "I'll go," I say.

"Bring her down, Morley," Mom says. "And warm up a bottle for her." I do the first thing and don't do the second. Lily just finished a bottle, not even 20 minutes ago. I wonder if my mother is sort of losing her sense of time? Or she just doesn't notice things?

She really isn't at all like herself. Even after Danny left and she cried a lot, she wasn't like this.

"OK, then," Aunt Eira is saying when I get back and pop Lily into her rocking seat. She looks around at all the women of her family, then gets very interested in the rattle toy on the rocker's tray.

Eira starts. "We're here today because we love you, Aoife" That's my mother's real name. Though it looks kind of odd, it's Irish, so it really sounds like EE-fa. Irish names always sound completely different than they look.

"And we are very concerned about you. You've told us you're always so tired, but you don't sleep. And you don't seem to have any energy. Or appetite. This isn't normal, even after a baby…"

My mother just looks at Aunt Eira, then finally says, "How would you even know? You've never had any babies."

Eira looks stunned, but ploughs on. "We want you to at least see your doctor. Get some basic blood tests. Just to rule out…something more serious than just being tired."

"What did your doctor say when you took Lily?"

My mother just looks down at her hands, loose in her lap.

"She didn't take Lily," I say.

"WHAT?" Aunt Sorcha says. She's been sort of half-listening for kid sounds from Daisy's room, but now she's totally focused on my mother. And looking like the shouting is going to start.

"OK. Let's get you there, as soon as we can get an appointment. I'll take you. And go in with you, if you want," Aunt Eira says.

"There's absolutely nothing wrong with me. Mind your

own business!" that's what the usual Mother would say. Or at least, my usual mother. She hardly ever bothers with saying things the nice way.

But that's not who's sitting in our living room right now. This is the sick mother. The kinda not-even-there mother. She just nods her head. "Alright," she says. "I'm heading back up." And slowly, like a very old person with a lot of aches and pains, she pushes herself up from the chair and heads back to the stairs.

After all the times I've been angry at my mother. All the times I thought I hated her. All the times she's been mean and unfair. Or she just didn't care about me at all. All those times...and now? I just feel sorry for her.

Because even I can see there's something seriously wrong.

The meeting pretty much ends there. Sorcha gathers up her boys, even while Daisy is protesting that they could have a sleep-over, pleasepleasePLEASE?

Aunt Eira says we need to talk. Meaning her and me. "About jewellery?"

"That and some other things."

"Like what?"

"Why don't we take these dishes out to the kitchen and talk there? I'll put on a movie for Daisy first. It's still too early for her bedtime. Could you bring Lily?"

I'm expecting Aunt Eira to want to talk about the jewellery orders, and what about some new designs? We're always doing new designs. That's to keep people interesting and coming back, my aunt says.

Instead, she wants to talk about heavy stuff. "I'll make the appointment for your mum and let you know. Don't worry about it." As if I don't have to worry about it. What if there's something big wrong with our mother?

"How is it, having Margaret here?"

You mean, your spy? Sam's friend, your housekeeper, our...what? Working guest? "She's been...OK. She's makes really good dinners."

"Well, that's something, isn't it? It always helps to get something good to eat. Better than that Christmas turkey I made, right?"

"I guess."

"And school? I hear you're getting some help with math? And going to a dance?"

Gosh. What doesn't she know about what goes on here?

"What about a dress? Would you like me to pick you up and we'll go into Halifax and shop for something? I bet Sam would like to come along, too. Say on Saturday, after the market?"

"Uh, no, I don't think so. I, uh, already got a dress," which is a big fat lie. "It's OK. But thanks."

She looks uncertain, but doesn't push it, for once.

"Well, then. Sam says to tell you she'd like to get together. Maybe help make some bracelets?"

As if she never even went off to New York to move to

Hawaii but ended up moving in with my aunt and almost-uncle. Like I wanted to do. She just stole the parents I wanted to have. Just took them for herself, after this ridiculous story about getting lost or something. And now it's all forgotten, like it never happened? No, I don't think so. "I'm pretty busy..." I say.

"I know you are, sweetheart," Aunt Eira says. "Try not to worry. We'll get your mother well again, do all we can. And meanwhile, Margaret and Gus are here to look after you and your sisters."

Right.

At school, everyone's still talking about the dance. Since I don't really plan to go, I kind of ignore it. Mainly, the girls are talking about who they're going with, besides their parent. Oddly, a lot of kids don't mind that it's a Parent-Student dance. They figure the adults will have one or two dances with their own kids, then they'll all stand around the edges of the room and talk or maybe even leave and come back later to provide rides home.

It seems like it's turned into no big deal, for most kids.

For me, not so much. I mean, it's OK to go with Uncle Gus. He's making all sorts of jokes about being an old dude going to a dance.

One problem is, what am I going to wear to this dance? Seabright has exactly three places where you might be able to buy a dress. One is a consignment store that mostly has pants and tops, boots and handbags and jackets that women buy to wear to work. That's where mom got all her work clothes, when she used to have a job.

Then there's this sort of gifty-boutique-y place that has stuff the university students buy. It's got a few racks of clothes, but nothing that would fit me. Everything there is crazy expensive.

The third place is a vintage clothing shop with hilarious old-fashioned clothes. Some of them are cute, but most of them smell funny, like they're full of perfume or hairspray. Our school is scent-free.

The other girls talk about how they borrowed something from their big sister, or they're going shopping with their mother, or their cousins. None of that works for me.

I look online, and read the reviews, and finally buy something with the credit card I use for my jewellery business. I'll figure out how to pay it back later. There's no way to know if it will fit right. It might be too long. I hope not.

It's a week later when it shows up. I try it on, and it's all sort of bunchy in the front, and too long, and not the same colour as it was in the picture.

Then, when I'm pulling it off, the zipper breaks.

And that's it. It's a bad luck sign, isn't it? It's saying, "Don't go to the dance!"

Instead, I'll stay home, like any other night. I'll read, or make jewellery, or do homework. Whatever.

No dance. Sorry. But, for once, Gus isn't being Mr. Easy-going about it. "What? No. You asked me to your dance, and I accepted. I'm delighted to go. Can't wait to go."

ARGGHHH. Even though I don't exactly remember me asking him. Wasn't it the other way around? It looks like there's no way to get out of it.

The doctor gives my mother medicine for depression that should help her feel more like herself and says the tiredness is probably just a bout of mono. Mono is like having the flu and makes you really, really tired all the time. The doctor says mum just needs rest, plenty of fluids and no stress. She says mono can take a long time to go away, but it always does on its own. You don't need any medicine for it. It's not anything serious.

Lily is totally healthy, but we need to change the type of milk formula she gets. The one we've been giving her is probably giving her tummy aches, the doctor says. That's why all the crying after she eats. We buy the special kind of formula and Gus helps me collect all the formula mix from our pantry, that's the kind Lily doesn't like, and we donate it to the food bank.

And it seems to work, at least for Lily. She cries a lot less. Mum doesn't come downstairs very much. She says she's dizzy. And so tired. And just not hungry.

"She just needs time to get better," Aunt Eira says.

"Rest is very good medicine," Margaret says.

I think something is wrong, but they don't. Neither does Aunt Sorcha, and she should know. She's a nurse.

Even so, I call Danny. It takes leaving three messages

before he calls me back. He says he already talked to Eira, and he's glad to hear Lily is OK, and he'll be down two weekends from now to get Daisy because she has another appointment with the audiologist. That's a hearing problems doctor. And he's pretty sure Daisy is going to need hearing aids.

He says don't worry, lots of people need help hearing, including kids. He says he's confident Daisy will adjust to using her new hearing aids and even enjoy being able to hear properly again. Maybe I can help her with more of the fish story? He says sorry, he has to go.

I see big trouble ahead.

Then, it's the week before the Dance, capitol D for Disaster.

Or, Gus says, "Delightful. Delectable. Devine!"

Aunt Eira stops around to see Mum and Lily. She's giving me and Sam a Mini-Girls' day at the spa before the dance, she says. We'll get new hairdos, a mani and pedi, a flower petal bath and then our make-up done while Aunt Eira gets a facial.

"No thanks," I say. I just can't do it, be all girly together and pretend like nothing's happened when I'm still mad at them both.

"I want to go too," Daisy says, top volume. "It's not FAIR. Morley gets everything! I want to be pretty and go to a dance."

Aunt Eira rolls her eyes, but then she just laughs and says, "OK, you can come with Sam and me to the spa. And then I'll bring you home and we can have a dance with Lily. How's that?"

Daisy looks uncertain. Then she brightens up. "I want purple sparkly nail polish on my toes," she says. "And green on my fingers."

Aunt Eira calls the day before the dance and says it's not too late, if I want to go with them on the spa day. I say I've got other plans. I don't, but so what?

Then it's that Saturday. Margaret's here with us all day, so I get a break from checking on my mother and babysitting Lily. That morning, I do our table at the market, with Sheila helping and we sell everything, but there are no pet portrait orders. In a way, that's a relief. To tell the truth, I'm getting a bit tired of doing them.

That afternoon, I do a bit of jewellery work, write in the Father Project book – this is actually book 5, so Dad is going to have a lot to read, when he finally does – and take a nap.

Then I have a bath, wash my hair and pull out the dress I bought. It doesn't look any better. I don't know how to fix the zipper, and I don't think I can just use safety pins to close it without it showing.

I look through my closet, even though I know what's there – jeans, tees, sweaters, one bathing suit, jackets and not much else. I have a jeans skirt and a couple of bathing suit cover-up things. I guess I could wear regular school clothes to the dance, even though it's semi-formal and at school they explained what that means. But I bet some kids will just wear their regular school clothes anyways. That's probably what I'll have to do.

Margaret suggests I look in my mother's closet. Mum's

always been slender and not much taller than I am now. I find a summer dress that's pretty, kind of a peachy-pink. It's more of a beach party dress than a go-to-a-dance dress, but it's only a little baggy on me. It's the best I can do. There's also a pair of cream flats that are hers, a bit big on me, but I stuff the toes with tissues. Good enough.

I model it for my mother. She laughs – the first time I've heard her laugh since – when? Before Christmas. Long before then. I want to keep her laughing, so I do a twirl. But then the laughing turns into coughing, and I run to get her a glass of water. "I'm just so worn down," she says, pulling the glass down after only one or two little sips. "But you look pretty, Morley. Have fun at your very first dance."

I'll try. "I will," I tell her. I can't tell if she heard me.

It's a couple of hours before the dance when somebody knocks at our front door. I hear Margaret get it, then she's talking to somebody. One of her friends maybe, I think, going back to sketching the view out my window. It feels good, restful really, to be drawing something that isn't a dog or a cat. Much as I love pets, I feel like I want to do more than just pets in my art. Not sure what more might be. This is just a sketch, more of a doodle really, not something anyone will ever see. Or pay for.

"Mor-LEEEE" Margaret calls up the stairs.

I hate interruptions. Especially when my head is really into a piece of art I'm making. But I head down the stairs anyways. "Someone here to see you," Margaret says.

Astonishingly, it's Mo. But this isn't an art lesson day. Why is Mo even here?

They looks at me, starts to smile, and say, "Looks like I got here just in time."

Mo puts her case down, turns me around to face the mirror next to our front door, and says, "This the way you're going to the dance?"

Um, yes. Why not?

"Come on," they say, grabbing their case and tote bags. "Show me where your room is. We have serious work to do!"

We do? "Uh, thanks. I mean, it's nice to see you, but I have to go out in, like, a couple of hours. And eat dinner. But I can ask Margaret if you can stay for dinner?"

Mo looks surprised, then grins. "Yeah. Sure. Let's get started, then see about something to eat. I'm not hungry, but you probably will need something. A sandwich, at least."

What? But then we're in my room. The terrible dress I bought is on my bed. I've got my mum's sundress on. There's some make-up – all that I own – on top of the dresser. It's just lip gloss and some freckle cream cover-up. I don't really like wearing make-up. It always feels itchy.

Feather is sitting on my bed, closely watching every move. He's always very interested in any kind of project happening. Otherwise, he'd be curled up for his major afternoon nap right now.

Mo starts pulling things out of their case and tote bags. Three pairs of shoes. A few things in clear plastic bags that look like fabric. A little case of jewellery. A whole lot of make-up. Brushes. Combs. A hair dryer. A lint roller.

"OK, Miss Star. This is your big evening, and I am your personal assistant. Also personal hairdresser, make-up artist and stylist. And we're gonna make you Red Carpet Ready, starting right now!"

Really? I'm so shocked, I don't know what to say.

"So, first, we're going to wash your hair..."

"But I just did that. Like, not even an hour ago."

"...wash your hair, with this, then condition with this, then styling gel, it's here somewhere ..." they say, holding up these fancy-looking bottles of products that look expensive.

"OK," Mo says, when I'm sitting in my red bathrobe, the one with stars on it, at my desk with wet hair wrapped in a towel. She looks at me, sort of squinting. "Hmmm...yes. Eye shadow, for sure, very pale. Just a hint of liner. And a touch of powder. You have lovely lashes. Yes..."

"Freckle-covering stuff," I say. "Because they're just ugly."

"Absolutely not," Mo says. "They're totally charming. If you've got real red hair, like you do, you're gonna have freckles. They're adorable!"

They are? But now Mo's saying, "OK, turn this way. Close your eyes. Lean back. Now, turn the other way.

Yes, good. Now, open your eyes, but not all the way open. Look up."

After a lot of that, it's the hair dryer. Then Mo is finger-arranging my hair in a kind-of updo. Held up with sparkly hair pins, but with bits hanging down. Then she's spraying something over my hair. It makes me sneeze.

There's no mirror, so I have no idea what all this looks like. Mo says I can look when we're done. Mo doesn't say how much longer that will be.

Finally, they step back, declare their work complete, at least from the neck up, and let me go in my bathroom to look in the mirror, and ...OMG!

I don't know who this girl is. She looks like my mother, a little bit, only really, really young. If she was dressed up like a Celtic princess.

"Um, I don't know..." I say. "Uh, make-up makes me feel kind of...funny."

"That's what happens when you use the cheap stuff," Mo says. "I never do. After all, it's what you're putting on your skin. Come on, let's look at some dresses. That little pinky one you've got is sweet for summer, but not for a big evening out."

Mo pulls out dresses – one after another, looking like something maybe Katie Perry or Taylor Swift would wear. Yikes! I mean, they're all gorgeous, but I can't even imagine wearing them in my own room. Wearing them to school – uh, no. Definite no.

There's a slinky sparkly gold one, one that's neon orange, one that's black with lace and a line of white and silver flowers along the hem, and one that's hot pink.

No, no, no and no I'm thinking as Mo holds each one up in front of me. Then I spot a plain blue one. "How about that?" I say, pulling it out of the pile.

"Hmm, maybe. Good colour on you. Kind of...old looking though. Like for your mother or something."

"I'm eleven," I say. "Everyone, just about, is older than me."

"Well, the idea isn't to look eleven, exactly. More like, say, 12. Or 13. You OK with that?"

Thirteen. A teenager.

"We're not trying to make you look like a grown-up..."

"Or a beauty queen."

"Or a rock star."

"Or..." Mo pauses, when there's a knock on my bedroom door. "Morley?" Margaret says.

Mo opens the door, and Margaret comes in with a big plate of chicken nachos and two cans of soda pop. "Oh, Morley. Very pretty. Like young lady. Murdo, so talented! Morley, Señor Gus say to tell you, time to leave soon. 20 minutes, he say. I tell him you almost ready."

"Sure, Margaret," I say. "Thank you!"

We eat and then I put on the blue dress, being super careful not to get any make-up on it. It looks good, I think.

"Good, not great," Mo says, frowning and then pawing through the dresses we haven't looked at yet. "Here, how about this?"

It's kind of blue and green at the same time, with a halter neck and a gathered swirly skirt that goes to just above my knees. It fits, but it seems more like it's floating around me, not like a piece of clothing I usually wear. I LOVE IT, even before I look in the mirror.

When I do, there's a smiling girl. A girl who looks like she's going to a really special party.

"Mirror selfie!" Mo says, getting in close and taking the picture with their phone.

Then I'm trying on the ballet flats Mo brought, choosing the ones with tiny stars on them.

"What about jewellery?" They open a box to show me some they've brought, mostly vintage costume jewellery.

I get out some jewellery I've made. Together we decide on a pair of blue drop earrings I made and one of Mo's costume pieces, a brooch with sparkly blue-green glass and crystals, pinned to the waist of the dress. She hands me a satin bag for the shoes and a little green evening purse. "For tissues, and lipstick for touch-ups, and well, I put a couple of other things in there, just in case."

Then I'm standing there, all dressed, holding the little evening bag and the pretty flats in their bag, and Mo says they want to get downstairs first so I should take three deep breaths, count to 25 and then come down.

I'm thrilled. I'm terrified. I don't know what you do at a dance or what you say. I should have thought of finding out these things. I think they talked about it in health class, but I wasn't really paying attention. Why? I don't know.

Another thing is I can't dance. I mean, with a partner. I know they talked about all the dance how-tos at school. When you should arrive (the time the dance is supposed to start, 7 p.m.) and what you should wear (shirts and ties or suits for boys and dresses for girls) and what to say if someone doesn't want to dance with you (just say "OK" and ask someone else. Don't get upset about it). Mr. Cadeau talked about the dances that are allowed and the ones you can't do. Dancing with anyone is OK, and so are circle dances. Show-off dancing isn't. Or rude dancing.

And I think there were some more things we needed to know about dances, but right now I can't remember what they are.

I count to 25 and make my feet walk along the hall, to the stairs and start down, clutching the railing.

At the bottom, Margaret, Uncle Gus and Mo are looking up at me. Mo is taking photos. Gus is grinning. So is Margaret. I'm not sure what my face is doing. I'm just trying not to trip and fall down the stairs. That would be so embarrassing.

Then people are saying, "You look lovely, sweetheart," and "Here's your coat; do you have your gloves? What about a scarf? And don't forget your shoes!" and "Have a really special time!" and Gus offers me his hand and opens the door.

nine

Too late to get out of it now.

ten

Gus hands in our tickets, chatting for a moment to the student taking them at the door before moving on because there's a line-up forming behind us. Then we walk straight ahead to the gym and through a tunnel lined with blue balloons to a room that looks like nowhere I've ever been.

It's still the gym. I know this. But it's also blue and green and silvery everywhere, even up on stage, where people are setting up the speakers, drums and microphones for the band.

This is called the Enchantment Under the Sea dance, so I was expecting a kind-of ocean-y look, but the grade eights or whoever did all the decorating have gone way beyond just sticking a few pictures of fish or whales or shells or something on the walls. They've made this whole underwater fantasy world. I wish Daisy could see this. She'd love it! I pull out my phone and start taking some pictures to show her tomorrow.

"Hey, Morley," Jayden says. Turning, I see Uncle Gus is already chatting with Jayden's mum, Dr. Van Haan. "You came, after all! Awesome, eh? It's like you're down south somewhere, like maybe Florida, isn't it?"

"Yeah," I say. I've no idea what Florida is like, or anyplace like there. "It's great. So creative!"

"Is that, like, your DAD?" a girl says, clearly not using her inside voice. I turn to see it's Tiffany. She means Gus. "He's like, ANCIENT! He could be Santa Claus!" She laughs, looking around to see who else is laughing with her. A couple of other kids kind of laugh, too. Adults act like they didn't hear.

"That's my Uncle Gus," I say, loudly, in Tiffany's direction. "Not my dad."

"Oh, right. Because your dad's really an astronaut, and right now he's up in a space station, circling the Earth," another girl, Karen, says. She was one of the girls who came to my sleep-over party. "Or, no, that can't be true because he's an Arctic explorer and he's way up North somewhere, searching for rare ice diamonds."

A few more kids have gathered around. Some snicker. Others are just waiting to see what happens.

"No, he's not..." I say. "Dad's just not here."

"Because he's really this famous movie actor in Hollywood and he's making a big movie right now and he couldn't get away."

"Wrong again, Kiera," I say, trying to be jokey about it and wondering why I ever invited her to my party. The truth is, I used to tell stories like these when other kids asked where my dad was and why he didn't pick me up after school or come see us play soccer or anything like that. "He's actually in a secret location, far underground, changing code to save the Internet from exploding and destroying the whole world."

I haven't told lies about my father since grade 4, but it feels kind of fun to do it again now. "So, my favourite uncle, Gus, has gallantly stepped in to take his place..."

Gus sends me a smile. He does look spiffy, like he's in one of those old-timey movies where, any minute now, he's going to start tap-dancing. Or maybe singing *and* tap-dancing. With his beard and mustache close-cut and his hair slicked back in a ponytail, he could be a rock dude, or maybe a grand-rock dude.

"Yeah, Morley, you're so full of stories, no one ever believes a single thing you say," Tiffany says. I decide to ignore her.

I spot Sam then, coming in with Dom. She has on the most amazing dress I've ever seen. It's shimmery green and has a sort of flower lace on the top and along the bottom of the skirt. Her hair is newly cut, very shiny black, and she has pale pink lipstick. It's like I've never seen her before. For the first time, I realize she's really pretty. Sam spots me and turns away to talk to some other kids I don't know. Grade sevens, maybe. Or eights. Since she started her accelerated program, I guess she knows a lot of people in the other grades, way more than I do or Jayden does.

Jayden, who also looks pretty amazing in a turquoise

shirt and red tie, starts to say something, but he's drowned out by our principal, up on stage asking people to please pay attention. That's Ms. Vida. She's tall and thin and looks great in her tuxedo. She welcomes everybody. She repeats the rules about no alcoholic drinks, no rowdy behaviour and students are to stay in the gym and not wander to other parts of the school. The dance will end promptly at 10 p.m., she says, and then thanks all the Parent Committee for organizing this dance and doing the spectacular decorations. There's LOUD applause.

Ms. Vida says a couple more things about there are drinks and snacks and we expect you to all be your best selves and have a wonderful night. Then she leaves the stage, the band people come on, the regular gym lights dim down and the whole room is dancing blue and green lights. Just like you were swimming, underwater, looking at exotic fish and beautiful corals.

It's magic!

The band gets going, Uncle Gus takes my hand and we're dancing. For the first hour or so, it's almost all adults dancing with kids, but then it changes, and the adults are mostly standing around the sides of the room, watching kids dance while talking.

Way more girls have come than boys, so there are girls dancing together and a couple of dance circles form. Of course, some kids try to shove other kids, the shier ones, into the centre of the circle, even though we were told not to do this. There's always someone that just has to be a rebel. Or a jerk.

There's a lot of jerky behaviour in middle school. More even than grade 5. I mostly try to ignore it.

This dance is semi-formal. That means a shirt and tie or a suit for guys and a knee-length, sleeveless party dress for girls. In homeroom, Mr. Cadeau handed out pictures showing what semi-formal clothing means with drawings of what it looks like for kids in middle school. For the dresses, halter top, high neck, one-shoulder or with straps are all OK. Strapless or too tight or your belly button or part of your bum showing or WAY too short is not OK. The guys can wear a suit, or just a shirt and tie with a good pair of trousers. Not jeans, or tees, or anything ripped.

You don't have to gender-dress. Girls can wear a tuxedo, for example, or boys can wear a kilt or other type of skirt.

Even with all the advice we got in health class about what to wear and how to behave at a dance, there's still one girl who came in a fake fur rabbit costume. I guess she thinks it's funny.

 A couple of guys are in school clothes and one boy even wore his gym shorts. And one girl, who for sure is going to get teased at school on Monday, is wearing sky-high heels and the kind of tight dress that she is sort of spilling out of.

Tiffany's dress is just about as bad. I'd be embarrassed if I had to wear it. And in those heels, I bet her feet are throbbing with pain. But she's keeping Liam for every single dance like she's glued to him. I see other girls sort of trying to get close to them, towards the ends of songs. Anybody can ask anybody to dance; it's not just boys asking girls like it was in olden times, like when Gus or Dom went to school.

Some of the girls seem to know all the correct moves to the songs, but most people are like me, kind of moving around and trying to figure out what to do with their arms. Not exactly dancing.

Slow dancing is only arms apart. If you don't want to dance, you can say so. If someone turns you down for a dance, it's no big deal. Ask someone else. Thank your dance partner at the end of the song. Avoid showing off, even if you are a good dancer. It's OK to dance with your friend group. Mr. Cadeau talked to us about all this stuff.

I want to ask Liam to dance. I watch for an opportunity. It never happens.

Some of the parents leave and it's almost all kids dancing. Jayden asks me to dance, a fast one, and then another, which is OK. When it switches to a slow dance, I tell him I need to leave for a minute. He looks disappointed.

I'm sitting in the washroom stall, when I hear some girls talking, I guess to another girl who just came in.

"You're so stuck-up, you think you're too good for everyone. People think you're a big fake, you're just so annoying. Why don't you transfer to another school? Or just go back where you came from."

It sounds like Karen who said this. I can't make out the other voices. Is she really this mean?

I could just wait another minute or two and hope they go away. That's what other kids did, when Julia was saying horrid things like this to me. They just watched and waited. Or walked away and pretended nothing was happening.

I'd like to do the same, but I can't. I gather up all that skirt, and get my pants pulled up again, flush, and come out of the stall and wash my hands.

"I can't go back to anywhere because I come from here. I was born here, at Kentville hospital. Just like you," Sam says.

I finish drying my hands and put an arm around Sam. "Ignore them," I say. "You aren't any of those things they're saying. You're smart and super talented and totally beautiful. Come on, let's get out of here."

"Girl crush!" Tiffany shouts after us. Then she says some uglier things, but who cares? She's the one who's the hater. Why is she like this? Who cares? That's her problem, not mine. Not anymore. Yes, I was bullied, and I got hurt, but I learned that bullies are nothing but liars. You have to stand up to them, but not alone. That's what friends are for. One of the things.

"Hey, thanks," Sam says. I notice that she looks kind of jittery, like those girls really bothered her. Sam is a really strong person, usually. Something to think about, later.

"Ignore them," I say. "They're probably just jealous because there's nothing special about them. Totally nothing. Bet they wish there was."

Sam takes a deep breath and says, "Want to go look at what they've got for snacks?"

I can hear the music. Another slow dance, which I'd rather avoid, but hanging out in the girl's washroom doesn't work. "Sure, OK." I've already had chips and a soda pop, but I get a handful of chocolate buttons. She chooses some cookies.

With so many people dancing, it's hot in the gym and I almost feel sorry for that girl rabbit. I'm pretty sure Jayden is going to ask me to dance again, and I don't really want to. I mean, with him. It looks like Liam isn't going to ask me. There's a lot of other girls trying to dance with him. Practically a line-up, as dances are ending. It's almost funny, but it isn't.

We go along the hall and sit on the floor, our backs to the lockers. Some other kids are doing the same, just talking and hanging out.

"I like your dress," I say. "Did you get it when you were in New York?" It's such a gorgeous dress, the kind of thing I imagine those New York girls get to go try on and buy anytime they want in all those fancy New York stores.

"I need to tell you something," Sam says. "It's about, well, when I was in New York. With Umma. When I said we went to galleries and shows and shopping, that was just all the things I wished we were doing. Like a fantasy, I guess..."

"You weren't doing any of those things?"

"No. It was just what I wanted to be true. I was always in our room practicing, or watching TV, or just waiting around for my masterclass with Madame, or for the auditions to happen."

Oh. Stuck in a hotel room, in a big city. Just waiting. It doesn't sound like fun. "What auditions?"

"To maybe get into a school that's all arts and music. Where my mother wanted me to go, instead of here. With a scholarship, because what I didn't know then was my mother lost all her money. I could only go to those schools if we didn't have to pay for it."

Wow, I think. No pressure, then. "So, you kind of knew your mum was having some kind of problems?" Mental health problems, I'm thinking. Like depression, only maybe even worse? And how do you lose a lot of money? Sam lived in a huge house with a pool and a housekeeper, that's Margaret. I always thought that Sam and her mum were rich. "Did she just spend it all? What happened?"

"It wasn't that I got lost or I forgot to get on the plane or anything like that. It was, well, there was something wrong. Really wrong, but I didn't know what, exactly. My mother was taking all these pills, and acting kind of weird, and saying she was super in love with this man in Hawaii who she'd never even met…"

"And she was just leaving you alone all the time?"

"Yeah. Pretty much. I found out she'd been telling some lies. Not just to me. To everyone."

"You didn't get on the plane because you thought something bad was going to happen?"

"Yeah. That's it. And then it did."

It did? "Was that, like, having ESP or second sight or whatever they call it when you can see the future?"

"No, nothing like that. Just – a really bad feeling of *wrongness*. Umma was acting so strange. I wondered if she was having some kind of – well, a meltdown."

"Like seeing people that aren't there or hearing strange voices in your head?"

"No, not that. More like, I think she was taking drugs. And drinking a lot. Both of those things together made her really kind of crazy in what she was doing. I couldn't depend on her."

"Because she was keeping secrets from you? Or telling lies?"

Sam nods. "Both. She had been, for a long time. But then it got...worse."

Wow, I think. That must have been truly scary. "So, you just decided to head back here, somehow."

"Right. But then, I got lost. Not just lost like wandering around."

"What kind of lost?"

She looks down, tracing a flower on her skirt with a finger. "I was kidnapped. I know that sounds – well, fantastic. Like a story. But it really happened. They were totally evil people. They'd kidnapped some other kids, too. Not just me."

OMG! Kidnapped? She's right. This is hard to believe. I look at her and see she's telling the truth. "What did you do then?"

"I waited til really late at night and I...well, I escaped. And ran. And, uh, got to the police and told them everything. They called your Aunt Eira and Dom, and my father. They found out what happened with my mother."

"That she got to Hawaii and found her new boyfriend?"

"Uh, no. She got upset on the plane. Really upset. They say she hit someone."

She hit someone? Wow. It's hard to imagine Ms. Park, who always looks so perfect like a model or something just losing it and hitting someone who's a total stranger. But maybe drugs could make you crazy enough to do that? "So, that's the part about she got arrested?"

Sam nods her head, "Yes."

"That's all, like, so strange, like one of your dad's movies." I look around to see if any other kids are close enough to hear. They aren't. Sam never talks about her father, who's a famous movie director who really does make Hollywood movies with celebrities like Keanu Reeves and Lady Gaga. Sam says she doesn't want kids knowing. She doesn't want to be the kid of a famous person, she says. I kind of get it, even though I'd love to be the kid of a famous person and maybe be kind of famous myself. Some day.

I ask more questions but Sam says she's not ready to talk about who the kidnappers are and where they took her and exactly how she escaped. And her mother. She says she still has some things to figure out about all that. In her own head. I can respect that.

"Thanks for telling me," I say. "I know it's private stuff. I won't tell anyone."

I guess I might have been wrong about some things,

about Sam.

"Can we be friends again?" she says. "I really didn't mean to steal your trip with Eira. It was totally an accident that I, well that I needed her to come and rescue me at the same time you were going to have your Girls' Getaway."

"She told you about that?"

"She told me how much she was looking forward to it, but sometimes, she said, life intervenes. I think that's like saying Bad Stuff Happens."

"But also good stuff. Sometimes. You got rescued. We get to go to this dance," I say, getting up and smoothing my skirt. "There might still be some candy on the snacks table."

"And we're still friends," she says, reaching out to hug me. "That means a lot to me."

Just as we get back into the gym Ms. Vida walks onstage to say, "This is the last dance. When this song ends, please collect your coats and have a safe journey home. Thank you, once again, to our wonderful Dance Committee for giving us this magical evening!" People clap, then the band plays. I take Sam's hand on one side, and Jayden's on the other and we join the circle.

eleven

"Cool dance?" Mo asks the next time we meet to do math. I hand them the bag holding the dress which I washed carefully after I found the directions tag sewn into it.

On the dance-with-Liam scale, not so much. But otherwise – Uncle Gus looked like he was having a great time, the music was cool, the gym looked totally amazing, so "Yes, it was. Thank you again for the dress. And the shoes and make-up and – well – everything. It was really kind of you. We had fun!"

"Glad you liked it. I have to give the dress back, but you can keep the shoes. They're too small for me."

"Give the dress back? Who to?"

"Friend in the city who owns a costume rental company. So, let's take a look at the math quiz you had to do yesterday..."

She laughs at my expression. No, I did not think Mr. Fafard was giving her my work to look at. I guess I accidentally say this, instead of just thinking it.

"Never mind frowning. He's trying to help you. So, Congratulations on getting the first five questions right!"

I'm totally surprised by this. It seems math teachers always want to tell you what you did WRONG. Mo says it's important to celebrate right answers and each step along the way to learning new skills, not just when you get all the way there. Mo says no matter what the subject, there's always more to learn. Best not to put off doing the celebrating, they say.

I'm not quite ready to see doing math the same as going to a party, but it's no longer my most disgusting and totally least-favourite subject, either.

Daisy comes back from a weekend with her father, and she's got her new hearing aids. They're tiny. They mostly go inside her ears with just a little pink part behind her ear, covered by her hair so you can hardly tell she's wearing them. I think they're kind of cute.

She hates them.

"STOP ALWAYS SHOUTING AT ME," she screeches, even though I talk quietly to her. Danny says they've been told the hearing aids will take some getting used to. Like glasses, he says, or like when I had a cast on my arm last year.

I tell Daisy another story about the fairy mermaids. Danny cuddles Daisy and puts up with her shouting and crying about the hearing aids. Everybody tells her to just be patient and they will help her. A lot.

She says they make horrible noises inside her head. And they hurt. And everything is TOO LOUD.

I feel so sorry for her, but what can I do? Maybe the hearing aids need to be adjusted or something? I don't know. I do know that Daisy turns them off, or takes the batteries out, or just doesn't bother wearing them. Not very surprisingly, a week or so later, she says she lost them.

When I say I'll help her look for them, she says she's never going to put them in her ears, ever again. She says they're the wrong ones. She can't hear the fishes sing or the whales tell their stories or anything like she wants to hear, she says. All she hears is cracketty racketty NOISE.

I don't know what to do to help her. Danny, Margaret, Gus, everybody says, "Don't worry about it. It takes time to adjust. Soon she won't even notice she's wearing them."

Maybe they're right.

Usually, Danny doesn't stay very long when he comes to drop off Daisy. On that Sunday he did, and then Aunt Eira and Dom with Sam, Aunt Sorcha and Uncle Chris and their boys all came in. Daisy brightened up when she saw our little cousins. Aunt Eira went upstairs and came back down with my mother, looking unwell, and they had Lily. The living room was pretty crowded with all these people.

Margaret asked Sam and me to help carry in a tray of sandwiches and another of drinks. By now, Margaret knows what everybody in our family likes.

When we got back to the living room, Daisy and the boys had gone to her room to play. Danny was standing, with Lily. Everyone else was sitting and talking. Sam and I thought we'd go up to my room, and Margaret was making her excuses about needing to do something in the kitchen, but Aunt Eira asked us to stay.

So, I thought, another family meeting. UGH!

Danny started off, explaining about the hearing aids and how they had to be cleaned every evening and the batteries checked and how we all had to help Daisy adjust to wearing them.

I had a hunch Daisy had already flushed them. I didn't say anything.

Then Aunt Sorcha talked about how after having a baby, and especially in winter, it's easy to just want to do nothing but crawl back into bed.

My mother, hunched in the rocking chair, looked embarrassed. And miserable.

"We all think it would be good to have something special going on. I mean, more special than just normal living," Aunt Eira says.

"Like a project," Dom says. "A day-brightener. Now that you've had, uh, time to recover. Mostly."

I look at my mother, who doesn't look recovered from anything. She looks older and thinner than I've ever seen her.

"Not that we're here to tell you what to do, Aoife,"

Uncle Chris says. "But we all think that you staying upstairs all the time isn't...well, it isn't healthy. For you. Or your daughters."

My mother just looks at him, as if she can't think what to say. She looks miserable.

"So, here's what we've got. Just an idea, Aoife. But you've got these baking orders, and only one part-time person to do them, with maybe some help from Margaret and Morley. And you've got bed-and-breakfast rooms, mostly empty right now. Can we agree on this?" Eira says.

Everyone nods yes or says it. My mother says nothing.

"And you need an income. In addition to your maternity leave and support money for Daisy and Lily from me," Danny says.

My mother shrugs. It's true. We do need money. It's the thing I've been worrying about. One of them. I know the school where she used to work (that was our school) must hold my mother's job open until the end of her mat leave so she can go back to it. That's the law. I also know she hates that job and doesn't ever want to go back. But if she doesn't, what will we do for money for groceries and oil for the furnace and gas for the car and for, well, everything? I guess I could do even more pet portraits and make even more jewellery to sell, but that still really isn't going to be enough to buy everything our family needs.

Everyone looks embarrassed when my mother doesn't say anything. Dom says, "So here's the thought. Leave the bed-and-breakfast, for now. There aren't many tourists this time of year anyways. Instead, move up there and turn this floor into a café. You could do breakfasts and lunches only, plus cookies or pastries and coffee in the afternoons."

People nod in agreement and Dom continues. "You're right on Main Street, there's plenty of parking nearby, people know you from the Saturday market, you've got the ideal location across from the park and the museum and just along from the harbour. Plus, Seabright has a couple of coffee places, but no real breakfast and lunch café."

My mother looks stunned, but finally, she has something to say. "I can see that you've all been talking about this. Behind my back. It sounds like a lot of work."

"That's our point," Aunt Sorcha says. "It is some work. We're all ready to help do whatever it takes to get you up and back on your feet. For your kids as well as for yourself. Gus, what would it take, in terms of renovation?"

"Well, I don't know," he says. "I'll give it a think. Shouldn't take much, I'd imagine. Maybe some wiring, put in a restaurant-style oven and dishwasher. Might need a walk-in fridge. Few other things to come up to code for a restaurant. And there's extra insurance you're going to need..."

"Sounds expensive," Uncle Chris says.

"Well, I guess we need to know exactly what it would cost. That is, Aoife, if this is something you want to do?" Danny says.

"I think, between us all, we can figure out how to do it

and how to pay for it," Aunt Eira says. My mother sends her sister a dark look. "A loan, of course," Aunt Eira adds. "Pay it back when everything is up and running."

My mother sighs.

"Why don't we all go away, think about it, look at how it could work?" Aunt Eira says. "Meanwhile, Aoife, I think we need to look at the orders and the money. Of all of us, Dom and I have the most time and we've already got businesses set up," she says. "Why don't we start there?"

"Are there enough orders to hire Sheila for more hours?" my mother asks. It's the first time she's shown any interest at all in anything besides just staying upstairs and sleeping, ever since she got home.

"Let's look at that tomorrow," Aunt Eira says.

Sam and I haven't said a thing. But then, no one asked us.

The good thing is the next day our mother does get up and come downstairs. She's dressed in yoga pants and a sweatshirt and her hair is clean and pulled back in a ponytail. She's pale and a bit shaky, but she's here.

I make her a strawberry banana smoothie, and she says it's cooling on her throat. She finishes almost half of it before she says she's just too full.

Aunt Eira and Dom take over the cookie business. Then it seems Shelia has an almost-full-time job at our house, because there are lots more cookie and cake orders.

Dom and Uncle Chris and Aunt Eira and I move all our stuff upstairs. They help me arrange it all so it actually looks like our home, not just stuff piled everywhere.

A new, huge stove and an even bigger oven get installed in our kitchen.

Aunt Eira, Dom and I pull out tables and chairs from the garage and paint them in beachy colours. We make up menus and posters about the café opening on Dom's computer. Gus builds a front counter and café-style tables in the two front windows.

In just a few weeks, the whole downstairs turns into a real café. We live upstairs. That's just until our new home, at Sea Garden, is ready for us to move there and turn the upstairs back into a bed-and-breakfast.

One day, I come home and find a big sign is up on the front of our home. Eva's Café it says. Breakfast, Lunch and Desserts. Open Thursday to Sunday, 8 a.m. to 3 p.m.

Then, one Saturday morning, it's our Grand Opening. I was worried that nobody would show up. Instead, it's mobbed. People are lined up out the door, right out to the sidewalk.

Inside, what used to be our living room now has tables and chairs. The walls are painted pale blue and have some framed photos I took around town and nearby, at the beach. There are also some of my pet portraits hung up. All the art is for sale.

Aunt Eira and Dom are always in and out, or else they're serving the customers.

Margaret is mostly here, looking after us. Baking.

Everywhere at once.

We don't sell at Saturday Market anymore, at least we don't go there, because the café is open that day and it's usually busy. Instead, the Happy Paws have taken over our table. They sell what they make and some of our cookies and cakes. They earn some money for selling for us, and we get more people interested in checking out the café. They also take orders for my pet portraits.

One day, I come home from school to find Dom in the kitchen, trying out what he says is a new recipe. It's Greek donuts. I didn't know there were donuts that are Greek. He says they're called loukoumades which is just a really long name for little honey donuts. Their housekeeper always used to make them when he was a kid.

I didn't know they had a housekeeper.

"Are you kidding? With 12 kids? Of course we did!"

Wow. Eleven brothers and sisters. I wonder what that would be like. I sure wouldn't want to be the oldest in that family! Imagine having to help out with that many younger kids and babies!

On the other hand, I guess you'd always have someone to talk to. Or borrow things from. And you'd probably never get lonely.

Sam giggles when I tell her about this. She says she'd love to have sisters, like I do. Or brothers, like Jayden has. She's holding Lily when she says this. I make a joke about great, you can have one of mine. She laughs, but it's a sort of being polite laugh, not a real laugh.

Another day, I get home to find Mo out in the kitchen with Aunt Eira and Mom. It seems Mo is going to work here now, on Saturdays to start and maybe more this summer.

"Oh, you two already know each other?" Mom says.

"From school," I say. "Mo is the one who's been helping me with math. And we did some drawing lessons together. And she helped me get ready for the dance, remember I told you about that?"

"I didn't realize," my mother says. "So, Morley, Daisy is on a play date with Jenevra and her mum has offered to drive her home after. Would you go check on Lily?"

I change Lily and take her to my room where I get her set up in her baby seat. She can almost sit up now. Soon, Mom says, we'll have to set up the playpen for her. I put on some music and have a look at my homework and talk to Lily. After a while, we get tired of that, so I take her for a walk.

In May, or as soon as our new apartment at Sea Garden is ready, we'll be moving there. Uncle Gus will also move there, to the apartment next door to us. Then this home will be entirely the café and bed-and-breakfast and I'll have to give up my bedroom. Again.

I guess it will be good to have a new place to live. I'll get my own room there and so will Daisy. It will just feel strange to go live in what used to be classrooms. They're the same ones where I was in Grade 3 and Grade 4. And we'll be renters, from Uncle Gus, who will be our landlord.

Another thing that will be different is Daisy will hardly ever be with us because she isn't wearing her hearing aids. She says she can't. And she won't. And we can't make her. There isn't a special class for kids who can't hear very good at our school, or any school near Seabright. For that, you need to be in a city, like Halifax, where Danny lives. She'll be transferring to that school, and then, except for vacations, she'll hardly ever be home in Seabright.

It feels like everything is changing. We're moving, and I love our house. As a house, not as a café and bed-and-breakfast. Daisy is leaving, to live mostly with her dad. Sam is back, but not in my grade anymore. Jayden is still my friend, kind of, but it feels like he's all about horses now and we hardly have anything to talk about.

Uncle Gus always seems to be at Sea Garden, seeing that the renovation work is getting done properly by the people he's hired.

Uncle Dom is turning into the King of Donuts for Seabright. Some Saturdays there are actual line-ups at our café to buy them. On those days, everyone works and it's mad crazy busy. He just laughs when people ask if he's "the real Eva?"

Mom is still nowhere near like herself. She comes down for maybe an hour or two at a time and does what she can which is never very much. Her name is on the café, or the name she usually uses because she says no one knows how to pronounce her real name when they see it written down. Mostly, it's Margaret,

Sheila and Mo who keep the café and cookie and donut businesses going. They're becoming like our family, we see them so much.

Aunt Eira, who was always the one on my side, is suddenly so busy, with searching for a new house to buy and selling her condo and planning her wedding and doing a lot for the café cookie business and organizing to travel to the piano and violin competitions Sam is in.

Even if Aunt Eira wasn't so busy all the time, I'm still mad at her. It seems like she doesn't even notice. Though maybe I'm getting a bit less angry than I was. She broke a promise to me, but she did it to go and rescue my best friend, who really was in trouble.

I guess I can understand that, or as much of it as Sam has told me.

At home, it's like everything keeps changing and changing. It's almost a relief each day to just go to dumb boring school. And here's the really odd part. I'm almost starting to look forward to lunch every day. The geometry part is not as bad as I thought it would be, because Mo makes it kind of a game. I don't like it nearly as much as English class or history, or even science, but even crabby old Mr. Fafard says he sees "some improvement."

So maybe not flunking math and passing Grade 6 is possible. It's almost the end of the school year, so I'm dreading that day when we get our report cards and I have to open it. And, worse, take it home. Margaret has already told me she expects to see it. And then it's just a matter of time when everybody knows what it says.

There are some things that should just stay being secrets.

twelve

For as long as I can remember, I've missed my father. Just wanting him there. Not only to take me to dances, or remember my birthday or buy me gifts at Christmas, or anything else I see Danny and other dads doing.

I want to know him. I want him to know me.

Do I look like him? Are his eyes the same colour as mine? What does he remember from when he was a kid my age?

Here is everything I know about him: His first name is Malcolm. He's Irish, like my heritage, like my great-great-grandparents were. They came from a place called Derry. I don't know what part of Ireland my father is from, or where he is now. I don't know when his birthday is, or what he looks like. I've never even seen a photograph of him.

Does he like swimming and art and stories and ice cream, like I do?

Does he dream of travelling to faraway places and having adventures, or has he already done that?

Is he handsome? Smart? Famous?

Is he happy?

Does he have a wife now and other kids?

Does he even know about me?

If so, does he ever think about finding me, the way I think about finding him?

The stories I made up about him, when kids would tease about why I didn't have a father, were all the wonderful things I could imagine him doing and seeing and being. He was off having a thrilling life, in my imagination.

My mother always has said she'd tell me more about him sometime. When I'm old enough to understand, she'd say, every time I asked.

But how old is old enough? I think I understand pretty good now. I'm old enough to look after my baby sister, old enough to have a business selling jewellery, old enough to save Gus from a fire and rescue Feather and do volunteer work at the pet shelter and serve our customers in the café and smile at them, even when they're crabby. I think I'm old enough.

One almost-springtime day in April, when the sun is out, I bundle Lily into her stroller and we walk all the way from our house to the other end of Main Street and back. On the way home, we stop at Scoops for milkshakes and a tiny taste of ice cream for Lily. She seems to like it.

When we get back, the house is quiet. I head up with Lily and find my mother is awake, sitting up in bed reading. She accepts her orange pineapple milkshake with almost a smile.

"How was your day?" she says.

I shrug. "OK, I guess. I got an A for my book report in English."

"Good for you," she says. "Have you made up with Sam yet?"

I didn't realize she even knew about that. "Yeah. Pretty much."

"That's good then," she says, sounding tired.

I don't want her to be tired all the time. I want her to be up, in the kitchen, making mountains of cookies if that's what she feels like doing, but just – being herself. Even when she wasn't really very nice to me, at least she was there, being a mother. Now, she's being, I don't know what. Just sick. And sad.

"I need to know," I say. "About my father. Who he is. Where he is. Why he isn't here, helping us. We need him."

She doesn't say anything, but at least she's listening. And taking tiny sips of the milkshake.

"I'm almost 12 and that's almost a teenager and I've started my period, which is starting to be a woman. Not a child. That's what YOU said. It's old enough to know who I am, who the people are I come from."

She doesn't say anything.

"And I have to know. I have to find him. I have to ask him some questions. And I think he should know about me. About us."

My mother nods her head. Just slightly.

How can you fight with someone who doesn't say anything but just nods as if they agree with you? It's so frustrating, it just makes me even madder.

My mother slurps her milkshake. She drinks nearly all of it. That has to be a good sign that she's getting better?

"You're right, Morley," she says, wiping her mouth on the sleeve of her sweatshirt. "It is time to tell you who your father is."

I'm so shocked, I sink down on the end of her bed. Luckily, Lily is already back in her crib. Sound asleep.

"I was just a bit older than you are now, 14, when I met your father. He was older, but still a teenager. We lived in Toronto, but we three girls, that's your Aunt Sorcha and Eira and me, came Down East to spend summer vacations with our grandmother every year. I think I've told you before, this was her house. She grew up here. Lived here all her life, almost."

No, I didn't know that.

"Was my father someone who lived here, back then, but from Ireland a long time ago, like you and your family?"

"No. He was from there, on a gap year, visiting an aunt and uncle for the summer. Having an adventure, I guess, before going to university."

"But you were younger?"

"Going into Grade 10. I had a part-time job, serving ice creams from a little stand in Clock Park. He didn't work, or maybe he did, helping his uncle in their store. I can't really remember. Anyways, he was..." she closes her eyes, as if she's back there. "He was very handsome and very popular. He had lots of Irish charm and that cute accent. All the girls wanted to go out with him."

"And you had a crush on him?"

She smiles. "I guess you could call it that. We all did. He had this sort of magnetic power. When he smiled, well...," she smiles, as if she's not just remembering, but almost back there, selling ice creams and seeing him telling her what flavour he'd like and if he wanted a waffle cone this time, or just a regular with two scoops. "I thought he didn't even notice me, even if he did know my name. He seemed to know everyone, very quickly. And everyone wanted to know him. Even your great-grandmother called him, 'That sweet boy.' "

"What was his name?"

"Malcolm. Malcolm Morley McNichol."

Malcolm Morley McNichol. From Galway.

"Did you go out with him?"

She reaches for her water and takes a sip. "No, nothing like that. There was – a couple of beach parties and some other times, but it was mostly a group of kids. Teenagers. Not my usual group of friends. More often, I saw him when he came to buy

ice creams. Nicky – that's what the kids called him --
loved root beer floats. Said he couldn't get them back
home."

Beach parties. Root beer floats. Kids liked him. And
I'm named after him.

But then I think – he was 17 that summer. Mum was
14. This all happened 20 or so years ago. I'm 11.

"He left in August," she says, her voice raspy. "On to
visit other relatives, he said. He was really excited
about seeing the Rockies. I was totally in love with
him by then, so I was devastated. I promised to write,
and I think he did too…"

"But you never heard from him?"

"Oh, I did, for a while. Mostly about seeing different
places. Then he went back to Ireland to go to
university. I was still in high school. He had other
girlfriends from that summer, I think. Or there were
rumours. And…well, life went on."

"But you saw him again?" She had to have. If he truly
is my father.

"I did. But I'm so tired now…" and I see she's gone to
sleep.

I'll just have to wait to hear more.

I go to my room and write down the story, so far. All I
can remember of what she told me. And then I write
questions: who were his aunt and uncle that he stayed
with in Seabright? Do they still live here? Who were
his best friends here, back then? Are they still around?
What about other girls he might have gone out with?

What else do I want to know?

Who are my other grandparents? Do they live in Ireland?

What about aunts, uncles, cousins?

What if I have more half-sisters, or half-brothers? Who are they?

Did my father go to university? Then what did he do?

Why didn't he ever come back?

I do a search on his name and find a Malcolm McNichol who lives in Scotland. There's another one who lives in Hong Kong and there's one out in Seattle and a couple of them in Los Angeles. I find out as much as I can about each of them, but none of them are the right age.

Then I think of course it's not going to be that fast and easy find him. If it was, my mother would have already done that, wouldn't she? She had a computer at work, and she has a phone. She could have looked on Google.

Aunt Sorcha must know something about him. Maybe Aunt Eira does, too. Sorcha would have been – ugh, more math – 11 when my father spent his summer here. Wow. Exactly my age now. It's hard to think of my Aunt Sorcha ever being a kid.

Eira would have been 9. Maybe not old enough to really notice who her big sister's crush was that summer. Could be worth asking. Even though I don't especially want to talk to Aunt Eira just now.

I know I have to talk to her sometime, and not just

about my mystery father. I send her a text. Wait. Send another one. Wait some more. Send her an email.

Still no answer.

I leave her a voice mail.

When Aunt Sorcha stops in, saying she's just here for a moment to check on us, she's in a hurry, I say I NEED to talk to her. And no, it can't wait.

When my aunt comes back downstairs and starts pulling on her boots, saying she just hasn't got time to chat with me, I stand between her and the door. "OK then," I say, "I'll talk fast. My mother is really sick. It isn't just like a virus that's going to go away. It's something more serious. I know it."

"You think you know more than the doctor? They said it's mono, so that's what it must be." She tries to reach around me to open the door. I don't move away to let her.

"You don't have mono for, like, months. And it doesn't make you lose a whole lot of weight. And not want to eat anything. And have pain in your hip."

"And how do you know this, Morley?"

"We, uh, learned about it in health class. Because it's mostly teenagers or young people that get mono. Not older adults, like mum. And you."

She laughs, but it's not a that's-funny laugh. "And, I suppose, you looked it up online?"

I shrug. Of course, I did. How else do you find out stuff?

"She doesn't want to eat. She doesn't want to do anything. I know the doctor said about depression, but I think it's more than that. She says she has no energy and she seems to be dizzy, a lot. Have you seen that she kind of doesn't walk the same way?"

"Look, Morley, you're worried about nothing. When you have a baby, you'll know what it's like, how tired it makes you. Now, I've got to go. I'll be back tomorrow evening."

I phone my other aunt, and this time, she actually answers.

"Morley, I'm kind of in the middle of something right now…" she says.

"It's important. Read your email. Answer it!" I say and hang up.

I text and email and call Danny. With pretty much the same message.

Then I go looking for Gus in his workshop. No luck. No use texting him. He doesn't know how to open a text. I'm not sure he even knows how to send an email. I call him. Leave a message. Hope he remembers to turn his phone back on, sometime soon.

Later, I find out he has a good reason for not answering.

I check on Lily again, change her, give her a bottle, and take her to my room til she falls asleep.

In the shadowy room, I think my mother must be sleeping, too. But she says, "Come in, Morley. Sit down. I'll tell you more of the story. About me and your father."

I sit at the end of her bed and get comfortable.

thirteen

"Your father was gone. Summer ended, and I went back to school,"

"Grade 10?"

"Yes. Not here. In Toronto. I couldn't stop thinking about him, even when I was going to class and seeing friends. Doing homework. Looking after Sorcha and Eira. Just having a normal teenager's life. But, all the time, in the background of everything there was…him. The way his hair sort of flopped over one eye. The spicy scent of him. The way his blue eyes danced. That smile. The funny things he said.

"It was like I ached for him. I watched the mail every day – people still sent cards and letters back then, even though yes, just about everyone had email by then. I thought he might write. Or call. Or…something. Visit Toronto even, maybe on his way back to Ireland."

"But he never did?"

I already knew the answer.

"Life went on. I finished high school. Grew up. Had other boyfriends. Nobody serious. Tried out college, but it wasn't really for me. Did an Office Assistant course. Got a job. Then a better one. Saved up my money and told everyone it had always been my dream to travel to Europe, for a few months at least. Maybe longer."

"Did you ever get to go?" I would love to travel. I had no idea my mother ever wanted to do the same thing. She's nothing like me.

"I did. Finally. When I was...oh, when was it? I guess I was about 21, maybe 22? Around there. I quit my job – well, I was going to quit anyways. There was a better job in my department, and they gave it to someone else who wasn't as qualified as I was, and I decided this really isn't what I want. The truth was, I really wanted to go back to college. Try again. But first, there was something I needed to do."

"Find Malcolm? Look for your great-grandmother's family in Ireland?"

"Both. And be on my own for a bit. Not just the same old routine every day. Freedom, I guess you could call it. I even had this crazy idea that I might like to stay in Ireland. Get a job there. See what that was like."

My mother coughs then. Takes another sip of her blueberry smoothie. Rests a moment. Continues.

She quit her job. She and a friend had it all planned out, backpacking around Europe and Great Britain and Ireland. They had their money all saved up, they had their passports, they had their tickets. They were going.

"Then my friend's boyfriend wanted to come along. I said, uh, no, this is a girls' trip, sorry. So, he proposed and she accepted." She shrugs. Takes a sip of milkshake. "I went on my own."

Wow, I think. That must have felt bad, like your friend betrayed you. And maybe a bit scary, travelling alone.

"I went to Paris, then on to Madrid. Spent a few weeks in Greece, moved on to Italy, went hiking in Germany and snorkeling in the Red Sea and shopping in Barcelona and met some people. Travelled with them for a while or went off for solo jaunts. Just went where I felt like going..." It's like she's back there now, remembering. Not here in this darkened bedroom.

Lily cries then. I check her diaper (OK) and bring her over to the bed, handing her to my mother, who gives her a cuddle. She's fussing, but she stills when my mother speaks again, staring up at her. Fascinated.

"It was always my plan to head back to Ireland, but first, I really wanted to see Scotland. See the Highlands. We have some relatives from there, too. I thought I might be able to find them. I didn't. But it was there, in a tiny little inn in a deep valley, just a beautiful place, that one of the other guests..." she sighs. Takes a sip of water.

"It was Malcolm. There for a wedding. One of his cousins. Unbelievable, I know. Such a coincidence! I thought I would look for him in Galway. That's in Ireland. And here he was, in the pub one evening when I went there for dinner, with some other people.

At first, I didn't believe it could possibly be him. I just...kept staring at him. Finally, they were leaving. I'd been sitting there, with a cold cup of coffee, thinking how can I get to talk to him – what will I say? Then, he said he'd catch up with the others and came over to where I was sitting, alone."

"What did you say, when you finally saw him again?"

"I don't even know that I said much of anything."

"Did he recognize you, like you recognized him right away?"

I was sorry as soon as I said it. He'd probably had all kinds of girlfriends and forgotten the ones from that summer all those years before.

"I didn't say who I was or how I knew him. Not really safe to chat up strangers in pubs for young women travelling alone..."

But he was my dad. Going to be my dad. Yes, I guess still a stranger to her. And me.

She continues. "We just talked. About oh, I don't know. About friends and school and his job and my job and life. He was so easy to talk to! And then they were cleaning the pub and putting the chairs on top of the tables and it was pretty clear they wished we'd leave. He walked me back to the little inn where I was staying..."

"And he kissed you?"

"Not – then. Later, yes."

They'd been together every day, at least for a meal, for all the days he was there. "And I fell in love with him all over again. I don't think I ever fell out of love with him...not completely."

"And he felt the same?"

"I think so. Back then."

"Did he remember that summer, when you were 14?"

"He said he did. Most of it. He said he remembered the Ice Cream Girl." She smiles as if remembering more than she's telling me.

"And then what happened?"

"I'm sorry, Morley, I can't go on just now. Let me rest." She hands Lily back to me to return to her crib.

Wow, I think. My mother fell in love with my father. Twice. And he probably fell in love with her.

I hope he did.

People finally start answering all the messages I've sent them. I say I'm so worried about my mother. I give them all my evidence. The weakness. No appetite. Losing too much weight to be healthy. She's really trying to be herself but has no energy. She moves like she's in pain. None of that really fits with having mono, except the tiredness.

I really hope there isn't going to have to be another family meeting to get my mother to the doctor. A different doctor, who maybe sees what I'm saying. And can do something to help my mother get better.

Not too surprisingly, Aunt Sorcha is all, "There's nothing wrong with Aoife that a good rest and not being pestered by Morley wouldn't cure." Fortunately,

Aunt Eira and Dom don't agree. They take Mum to a different doctor. The new doctor orders a bunch of tests. Aunt Eira takes Mum to get all the tests done.

Then, we wait.

I wonder what happened next with my mother's love story. She must have gone on to Ireland, like she planned, and met up with him.

On another afternoon, with a vanilla banana smoothie, she tells me how they went to museums, and shopping, and to restaurants – all the things they do in those movies about falling in love.

"What did you find out about his life? What he was doing, all those years?"

"He went to university, then law school. He had a girlfriend and almost got married, but then she married someone else. He travelled. He worked for a few different places, then in his family's business..."

"What was that?"

"They owned some stores. Like small department stores. Mostly in Ireland."

"Did he like doing that?"

"Not so much. He said he always planned a different life. He never wanted to go to law school, but his parents put a lot of pressure on him, so he went. He was a lawyer but didn't enjoy it. And working in retail was just a job."

"What did he want to be?"

She laughs, but it turns into coughing.

I wait til it passes.

"An artist. He said he knew that was ridiculous. You can't make a living as an artist..."

"You can if you're Banksy. Or Robert Bateman." Or, I think, me.

"We had fun. A lot of fun. And then..."

Oh no, I think. It ended. He was already married. Or he had another girlfriend. Or...what?

"He asked me to marry him."

"But you didn't want to?"

"I said, 'Yes.' "

Oh...but why...?

"He went to tell his family about our plans. I waited, back at the bed and breakfast where I was staying. I wanted to go with him, but he said no, wait here, I'll be back soon. So, I waited. I waited there for days. Then a week. Two weeks."

"He never came back?" Just like after that summer in Seabright.

"No. He never came. I searched for him. I went into all the department stores his family owned, in Galway, and Dublin and even in Belfast, looking for him, asking for him. They didn't seem to know who I meant."

"What about his family? Did you ask them?"

"I'd only met one of his sisters, just the one time. She wasn't very friendly. I went to the door, what I thought was her house, but she said to leave, I was harassing her. She threatened to call the Garda. That's the police, there."

Imagine being alone, deserted by your boyfriend, searching for him and no one wanting to help you. It was so sad.

"I looked everywhere I could think of. Then, I was starting to feel – odd. I'd seen Ireland and loved it. Loved being there. It's such a beautiful place. But I felt sick, and went to a doctor, and she said, 'Do you think you might be pregnant?' And she was right, I was."

"With me."

"Yes. I felt so alone. I came home. Not to Toronto. By then, your grandfather...well, I didn't want to be there, even though I missed Sorcha and Eira. But Sorcha was going to nursing school by then and hardly ever at home and Eira was a teenager, way more interested in being with her friends than her family. I visited for a week or so, then came here. To your great-grandmother and your great-aunt. Here in Seabright. They were wonderful, so good to me and excited that there would be a new little baby. I got a job and worked til you were born. And the whole time, I wrote to your father. Missed him. Tried to find him."

"But he never answered?"

"It was as if he had simply vanished the day he went to tell his family about us."

"Why didn't you go with him? That day?"

"He didn't want me to. He said it wouldn't be long before he'd be back, and we could be together. I think possibly things weren't that good with his parents."

And then I see she's crying. I put Lily back in her crib, and I sit on the side on the bed, lean over and hug my mother.

Feeling alone. Betrayed and abandoned. Not knowing what happened. Or why.

Lied to.

And there are secrets you can't find answers to.

I know how that feels.

fourteen

Uncle Gus calls me from the police station to say not to worry, he'll get home when he can. Tell the others.

Someone broke into Sea Garden overnight, did a lot of damage and stole tools that belonged to Gus or the construction workers he has turning our old school into condos and apartments. He says he's angry about it and I don't blame him.

How unfair that is, to be doing something good for our community like making new homes for people and haters just try to trash it. I know how much this project means to Gus. He knows what it's like to lose your home.

And then I remember we're supposed to move there as soon as our apartment is ready so that the upstairs of our house can be turned back into a bed-and-breakfast. I've seen how many guests we usually get in summer and I know how much they pay to stay with us. It all adds up to a big part of the money for our family. It's much cheaper for us to rent at Sea Garden than live here and not have the money from our bed-and-breakfast guests.

There are already bookings for those guests, so soon, we have to move out. But to where, if Sea Garden isn't finished? Could this make us homeless, too?

It's late afternoon, so all the people racing around selling cookies, cakes, bars and squares and gadzillion donuts to crowds of customers is done, at least til tomorrow. Mum and Lily are asleep. Daisy is colouring pictures of fairy mermaids I drew for her. So there don't seem to be any "others" to tell just now. At least not here.

I try to think of who will need to know. Or want to know. Aunt Eira and Dom. Aunt Sorcha, I suppose. Danny? I decide yes, since this is Lily's and Daisy's home we're concerned about, as well as mine and Mum's.

I send all of them pretty much the same text. Tell them no details, I don't know yet. Get Lily, put her in her stroller and bribe Daisy into coming for a walk with a promise of a stop at Scoops and yes, she can have sprinkles on her cone.

By the time we get back from that and I put Mum's salted caramel milkshake in the fridge because she's still sleeping, everybody has texted back:

Aunt Eira: *WHAT? Is Gus OK? If he's in hospital, tell me NOW!*

Me: *No injuries. Damage to the school. Tools stolen. Gus at police station now. That's all he told me.*

Aunt Sorcha: *So where are you now? I hope you weren't with him!*

Me: *Home. As usual. All OK here.*

Danny: *Tell Gus Sorry to hear about. Will be there tomorrow to pick up Daisy. See what I can do to help then.*

Aunt Eira: *You're sure you're OK?*

Me: *We're fine. It's Uncle Gus I'm worried about.*

Aunt Eira: *I'm coming over. Hold on!*

A few minutes later, Aunt Eira and Sam walk in. I'm glad to see them. I can look after all of us, but I don't like doing it alone, especially at night. Even though it isn't even dinner time yet, it's already getting dark out.

My aunt is upstairs with my mother for a while. When she comes back down, Sam is in the rocking chair, giving Lily a bottle. I'm helping Daisy with her reading, which is behind everyone else in her class, so her teacher sends home books for us to read together every evening.

I'd like to ask Aunt Eira about the Girls' Getaway weekend. If we'll ever have it. It still hurts that she doesn't even see how much it meant to me. It's like how much I was counting on going doesn't even matter to anyone but me.

She's got a text from Uncle Gus saying he shouldn't be much longer. She puts the dinner Margaret left for us (a pan of quesadillas) in the oven to warm, makes tea for us, and sits down to talk about what jewellery she needs me to make next. I say I want to make less jewellery. Not stop completely, but make less, because with looking after my sisters and Mum sick and school and the café and everything, I don't have much time for myself. None, really.

She says with selling her condo, looking for a house to buy, getting Sam settled with her and Dom, planning their wedding AND the Eva's cookie-donut business, she absolutely gets it about having no time.

"It's just a hard time, Morley. There's too much going on. Your life is pretty good, most of the time, isn't it?"

"I guess. Yes."

She pours my tea, then hers. "We all go through bad times, but then, life gets better. The sun always comes up. You just need to hold on for it a bit longer. That's all. We all do."

"Right."

"OK, I know, not terribly original. I saw it on a British detective show on TV. But it's still true."

I know she's trying to help me feel better. "Where will we go, Mum and Daisy and Lily and I, if we can't move to Sea Garden next month, like we were going to?"

She doesn't hesitate. "You'll come to live with us. Dom and Sam and Margaret and me, at our new house," she says, as if everybody had already discussed it and nobody even needs to ask this question.

"You're buying a huge house?"

She laughs. "We'll double up on bedrooms if we have to. Make it work. Now, go upstairs and see if your mum is coming down to have a bite to eat with us?"

Lily is in her baby seat, watching Sam with that complete staring that only babies can do. Sam is at the piano, playing something. One of her competition pieces, I guess. Daisy is in her room, headphones on, listening to the mixtape I made for her for the ten-zillionth time. Mom is awake. She decides to come down. She says she wants to talk to Gus about something.

Gus comes in, looking upset. There's seven of us, with Lily in her baby seat and everyone else crowded in around the table, eating and all talking at once. The mess at Sea Garden will set them back a couple of weeks, at least, Gus tells us. Plus, there's the nightmare of all the insurance claims. He doesn't expect the police to be able to do much. But it could have been worse.

Mom, sitting quietly until now, is pushing one little bit of food around her plate. I get her espresso milkshake from the fridge and hand it to her. She smiles a thank you while Aunt Eira frowns. "You need to be eating something more nutritious than that, you know," she says. "You need to build up your strength!"

"Stop it," Mum says, but softly. Then, incredibly, she makes a joke. "You keep that up and you'll turn into Sorcha!" Aunt Eira looks a bit embarrassed, and everyone laughs. Poor Aunt Sorcha, not here to defend herself. But it's true. Mum is the oldest of her sisters. Like me. If anybody gets to be bossy, it's the one who's the oldest, because she is the one who has to look after the younger ones. But now, it looks like, they're looking after her.

Mum sips on her milkshake and she's smiling. "So, Gus," she says when the conversation stops for a moment, "what happens now? I mean with Sea Garden?"

"Better security. I'm getting more outside lights installed and putting up a couple of CCTV cameras. And I think someone has to be there, so once I've got my workshop set up there and my place finished, or good enough, I'm going to move in. Get a guard dog too, I'm thinking."

"Oh..." Mom says. So, we'll be here alone. And Uncle Gus won't be paying any money to our family to live upstairs. It's not good news.

"Then, first place to get finished will be yours, Aoife," he adds. "Just like we planned. Except maybe a few weeks later than we hoped. I'm sorry."

"Not your fault," Mum says.

"So come to ours," Eira says. "You and the girls. And Margaret, of course."

"Your condo? But you already have things piled up everywhere and just about no space."

"Well, that's the thing. We've received a good offer on the condo, it's just getting down to negotiating the conditions. I think we've found our buyers. And we've put an offer in on a place up on Ridge Road. With probably more space than we'll ever need. We should hear on that by tonight."

Mum just nods her head Yes.

"It has a garden. And a view. Plus, a lot quieter than

here."

"But what about the café? And the bed-and-breakfast?"

"Well, we've got Sheila and Mo working with us now, and we'll probably need to hire a couple of other people, plus Dom and me. You, when you feel up to it. We can hire more as it gets busier."

"Yes. I see," Mom says.

"Don't be concerned about it. We'll figure out the moving and getting the bed-and-breakfast spiffed up and ready for guests, and...well, all that," Eira says.

In addition to planning her wedding. Getting Sam to her violin and piano competitions. Selling stuff online, as she does, and Dom doing whatever it is he does online. I've never figured it out. I do know that he created software that he sold the rights to when he was 17 and made so much money he never has to work again.

Later, after I've read to Daisy and she's gone to bed, Sam and Aunt Eira have gone home, Uncle Gus has gone off to his room to deal with hiring a security company and getting more lights and cameras installed at Sea Garden and something more to do with the insurance, I take Lily up and sit with Mum.

"A lot to think about, Morley," she says. "Do you want to live at your aunt's? Could be nice, with Sam there."

"I suppose. Not like here. I like our home."

"I do, too. Always have. It has a lot of memories..." she says. "But maybe it's time to try something different?"

We sit there, not saying anything. Thinking.

"Pull out that bottom drawer of my dresser. Near the bottom, there's a red book..." she says.

Buried under her sweaters, I find a leather-covered book. Of photographs. I hand it to her.

She runs a hand across it and smiles.

And opens it.

And that is when, for the first time, I see what my father looks like. Used to look like, when she knew him.

At the beach, with other teenagers.

Eating ice creams. You can tell it's in Seabright, on Main Street. Just a few blocks from here, at Clock Park. Or at Kingsport Beach. Or at The Lookoff.

Laughing together.

And then there are more, but my parents are older. No longer teenagers. You can still tell it's them. She has long, straight blonde hair and wears dresses. He is tall, with reddish-brown hair and blue eyes, like mine. You can see they're happy together.

"But didn't you have digital cameras back then?"

"We did. But you could still get prints made, or do them yourself by then, if you wanted them in a book. Like this."

"Why would you?"

"Well, because you can lose your phone, or forget you

even have photos on your laptop or wherever. I like having them in a book you can hold. And flip through."

And remember.

And tell the stories, when the pictures make you remember.

He made her happy.

But he left her. Twice.

Why?

I decide that I have to find him. I have to ask him these questions. I have to see his face, when he answers.

I have to know. And I think my mother needs to know, too. She just doesn't know how to find the answers, and she's too proud or something to ask somebody who maybe DOES know how to find him to get hold of him. Somehow.

Somehow.

How, exactly?

I have to think about it.

Because she misses him. She still loves him. She's always loved him. Even after what he did.

I'm not sure that I love him, or even could forgive him for leaving us. But I'd for sure like to find out why he did.

I ask my mother if she wants the red book close, on her bedside stand where she can reach it, but no, she wants me to put in back in the bottom drawer, under all the sweaters. When I do, I notice another, smaller, book underneath it. I see that she's tired now, so I don't pull it out. Or ask about it.

I'll do that another time.

Later, the house is quiet. I can't sleep. I sit at my desk, writing. Thinking. Drawing a bit. Mostly sitting, looking out the window at the stars. Wishing a comet would go by, so I could make a wish.

Why didn't my father do what he'd promised and come back to marry my mother?

Why didn't my mother do more to find him? If he'd changed his mind about being with us, well, at least she'd know. I'd know. It wouldn't always be this wondering why, why, WHY?

Why he would just leave, like that?

Why can't other people change to be who they really should be?

My mother would get up, get dressed and fix her hair and put on pink lipstick, just like normal. She'd go bake a pile of cookies and sell them, and some cakes, too. While smiling, because she wasn't sick or depressed anymore.

Daisy would stop shouting and just put in her hearing aids. Then she wouldn't have to move away from us to go to a special school.

My real father would turn up. And my parents would be in love and happy together. We'd be a real family, just like I've always wished for and wanted.

Uncle Gus would get his Sea Garden homes finished and we'd move in, and it would be great to live there.

The bed-and-breakfast and the café would be even more successful. We'd never have to worry about money again. Or having a real home.

Jayden wouldn't be so sad and kind of cranky, most of the time. I don't know what's really bothering him. He won't say. Except, I know it's not about the horse business he has with Patrick. He always brightens up when I ask about that.

And Lily – well, she's almost sitting up now. And she's happy, most of the time. I guess she's got what she wants, which is lots of people to cuddle her, rock her, take her for walks, give her warm milk, sing to her and just generally love her. Like me.

But then, she's still little. She doesn't know there's so much more to get. And to want, whether you need it. Or you don't.

But I think that if it's about your family, you do.

fifteen

Mo works at our café now. They're already there, helping make cookies or donuts or something and serving our early customers when I get to the kitchen every morning on the days when the café's open.

This means no tutoring with Mo at school lunchtimes. Instead, I sit with some new friends. Usually that's Callie, DeeAndra, Tyler, Ryan and Sian. It's not the same as it used to be, with Sam and Jayden. But it's OK.

Mo stays after her work shift at our cafe most days, so we can still work on geometry when I get home from school. Mo says we need to work together to get it untangled for me. And, amazingly, they're right. I don't get As on math tests, but I do good enough to get Cs, and once I even got a B on a test. Pretty amazing, I think. Good enough that Mr. Cadeau says he's really pleased to see my progress. He sends a note home to my mother that I don't mind giving her.

Mo wants to see more of my jewellery, so I show them. That leads to wanting to see my art, too. I get that out.

"So, do you only draw animals, like pets?"

"Yeah," I say. "Pretty much. Except for the ones down in the café of scenes from around here. Tourists seem to like them."

"How come? Haven't you ever wanted to draw other things?"

I shrug. "Like what?"

"Well, like people. Like a drawing of yourself. Or maybe your sisters. Or me?"

"You want a drawing of you?"

"Sure," Mo says. "Why don't we do a swap? You do a drawing of me I can send to my mother for her birthday. And I'll do a haircut and make-up for you. Or anyone you want, as a gift from you. What do you say?"

"My mother," I say. "It was her birthday. In January. But I didn't really get her anything, except just make her a card."

"Well, we can do better than that!" Mo says, hugging me. That's what we do. I make another card for my mother. It doesn't say Happy Birthday – that was a few months ago. Instead, it says, "Hope You're Feeling Better Soon." On the front, I draw a picture of her. In the drawing, she's the mother I remember, from before last year, before Danny left, before we even had the bed-and-breakfast or she sold cookies or we met Gus. Inside, I tell her how much I want her to be well and happy. I tell her about getting a new hairstyle and her make-up done, when she wants, from Mo.

Mum looks at the drawing, reads the words inside and cries. And hugs me. And makes a joke about how she's really crying because she read the note from Mr. Cadeau about me and my geometry.

Then the doctor's office phones. Aunt Eira answers. The doctor's receptionist says that my mother needs to come in for a conversation with Dr. Singh. Today would be good. Now, if possible.

They go right then. They aren't gone very long. When they get back, I can see that they've both been crying.

Why?

"We need a family meeting," Aunt Eira says. "I'll start calling people. Morley, you can help your mother."

"What's wrong?" I want to grab my aunt, shake her, make her tell me.

My mother sinks into her rocking chair. "It's cancer," she says.

Cancer.

My mother has cancer.

"NOOOOO," I scream. "Nooooo. It isn't true. It can't be." And now, I'm crying too. Sobbing.

It is true.

Everyone comes. Sits. Talks. Looks sad. Or cries.

Finally, they leave.

"I'm going to do all the treatments. Do everything they say. I'm going to fight this, Morley," my mother says as I sit with her that night, neither of us able to sleep. "I'm going to do everything I can to get better to be with you. And your sisters."

I still go to school. Still look after Lily and Daisy. Still walk and talk and look like Morley in the mirror, but it's all a big act. I don't feel like Morley. I feel like kind Zombie Morley. Or maybe hollow Morley. The regular Morley is kind of floating above me, watching me, making comments like, "That was really dumb. Why did you do that?" and "Get up. Get washed. Put on clothes. Eat some toast. Feed Feather. Help Daisy. Check on Lily."

It's like every single thing I have to do I have to tell myself to do it. Make lists in my head of the next things I have to do. I feel like if I don't, I'll just turn into dust or smoke and blow away.

Zombie Morley does homework. Brings milkshakes home for her mother. Asks Uncle Gus to write some fairy mermaid music for Daisy. He likes funny songs. He's good at playing the piano. Maybe he can make up some happy songs for her. She doesn't really understand what's going on. She just knows Mom doesn't feel well and has to take a lot of yucky medicine. And go to the doctor.

Zombie Morley makes more jewellery for Aunt Eira. But not a lot. It just feels so hard to even care about making jewellery, or doing art, or writing stories, or reading books, or watching YouTubes of silly cats, or making pet care videos, or any of the other stuff Normal Morley does all the time.

It's like every little thing takes so much energy to do. Like everything is just too hard. Even breathing is hard.

At school, I don't tell people. I don't want them to know. I can't stand them acting all sorry for me.

Sam knows, because she lives with Aunt Eira and Dom now. Jayden knows, because I told him. Margaret, Sheila and Gus know and so does Mo. I guess Aunt Eira told Mr. Cadeau, because he said if I need time to be home with my family, I can do that. He'd bring my schoolwork to the house, he said. And Mo could help me with it, if I wanted.

I didn't. It seems better to go to school. That probably sounds dumb. Usually, I'd be happy to bag off school if I could. Now it's harder to be home.

My mother and I talk, every night just about. About my father, her soulmate, that's what she calls him now, reminding me that I have to find him.

I don't tell her that. I don't want to make her all excited about seeing him again til I'm sure that will actually happen.

We talk about our garden, and what it could look like this summer, with picnic tables in it for the café customers to sit at while the eat their sandwiches or whatever we make for them.

We talk about our new apartment at Sea Garden. She wants her room to be painted pale orange, her favourite colour. And blue for the living room.

We talk about Aunt Eira's wedding. What sort of dress do I want to wear? What do I think it will be like, all of us going to a fancy big wedding in the city?

We talk about Daisy and her hearing aids. How can we get her to give her new ones (because we never did find her first ones) a real chance to work?

We talk about Lily. Getting big so fast! It won't be long before she's crawling around and eating real food!

And, sometimes, when she wants to, we talk about places she went to, when she was travelling. About what it was like, to be in the big cities in Europe. Or the Highlands, in Scotland. Or different places in Ireland.

She tells me about what it was like. She says they have fairy trees there. And magic wells. And pubs, everywhere, with fiddle music and people dancing. Just like a ceilidh here with all the singing and carrying on.

When people hear that she's sick, they send flowers. Big bunches of tulips and daisies and lilies come from Danny, her friends at Saturday Market and people she used to work with, when she had a job. She says she doesn't want them. It's just too depressing, watching beautiful flowers dying, she says. I show them to her and she reads the cards. Then I take them down to the café and arrange them. At least the customers might enjoy them.

I get the picture Danny took of Lily, Daze and me printed and put it in a frame and give it to my mother. We hang it on the wall, where she can see it from her bed.

Gus plays silly songs for Mum to make her smile and, together, we make her mix tapes of her favourite tunes. We bring her books and magazines and binge recordings of *Downton Abbey, Murdock Mysteries* and *Project Runway*.

Aunt Eira sells her condo. She and Dom and Sam choose the house they want to buy and after some back and forth, they get it. They organize all the moving out and moving in, even while organizing their wedding and keeping our cookie-donut business going. Mum says she just doesn't know how they do it. AND they're both taking my mother to all her appointments. She has to take a lot of pills and meal supplements and do something called Immunotherapy every day for two weeks. Once her strength is built up some and she gains some weight, she's going to have to do chemotherapy.

I've read everything I can find about it online. It sounds really horrible.

"I can do this," my mother says. "I have three really good reasons to want to get better and live for a long, long time. Til you're a little old lady," she says, "and I'm totally ancient!" It's good she can make a joke about it.

I can't.

Uncle Gus writes fairy mermaid music for Daisy and tells her she has to wear her pink shells if she wants to hear it.

Jayden tells me the reason he's been so unhappy

lately is that his dad wants them to sell everything, including all their horses, and move to Australia. Jayden's mother doesn't want to move to Australia, or anywhere else. She says her home, her friends and her vet patients are all here. Jayden and his brother, Patrick, are happy here. There's been a lot of fighting at their house, ever since Christmas when his father announced that they were selling up and moving.

"He didn't even ask anybody if that's what we want to do," Jayden says. "Sometimes I get so mad at him!"

"What do you think's going to happen?" I hope he isn't leaving. Australia is so far away. Too far to visit.

"Dunno. Kids don't get a vote in these kinds of things."

"What do you wish would happen?"

"Nothing. Things to stay the way they are. Were. Before Christmas."

Yeah. Me too.

In Eira's and Dom's new house, Margaret gets her own apartment, Sam gets her piano back at last and doesn't always have to use a little electric keyboard to practice, and my mother gets a pretty bedroom that looks out towards where the garden will bloom next month, when it's finally Spring.

I've stopped even caring what I get. I share a room with Daisy because she's become scared of the dark and wants to climb into bed with me most nights. I let her.

Sam tells me a bit more about what happened when

she was in New York City. Not all of it, but a bit more of it. I think she was so brave!

And my Aunt Eira went to save her. And bring her home.

I was the one who didn't do one single thing to help. Instead, I ghosted her. I'm so ashamed. I've apologized. But that's just words, and sometimes words are not enough. I made her some art – a drawing of her with Aunt Eira and Dom. And bought some cute sheets for her new room, with music notes on them. And a duvet to go with them. This is still not enough to make up for what I did, or didn't do, but it's a start.

The Girls' Getaway Weekend finally happened. Sheila and Mo and the two university students we hired part-time kept the café going and looked after the bed and breakfast guests so we could go.

On that weekend, Aunt Eira was supposed to go do some sort of wedding stuff with Dom's mother and a couple of his sisters. I think they were going to look at wedding dresses or taste samples from the dinner menu or some other thing brides have to do but there was some sort of big family blow-up about it.

Aunt Eira looked pretty stressed out about it, so I didn't ask for any details.

Sam heard Aunt Eira say something like "three-ring wedding circus" and "35 thousand and that's just for the band? And $150 a plate for the meal? That's total insanity!" and, Sam said, some other things you might not expect your aunt to say. Even Sam, who's heard a lot of bad language from other musicians at rehearsals, plus, she says, from her mother, was shocked. The way it ended up was Aunt Eira threatened to cancel the whole wedding. Dom, who really wants to be our Uncle Dom, took her out for dinner, just the two of them, just to talk. Where it ended up is the wedding is still going to happen, but here, in Seabright. In the garden at their new house. Or at Eva's café, if it looks like it might rain.

"Just you, me, our best friends, your family, whoever from my family wants to come. It'll be perfect. Far better than some big production in the city," is what Aunt Eira told me he said.

I think that's so romantic. And it's going to be a garden wedding, in June which is the most beautiful month, gardening-wise, of the year. That's not just my opinion.

So that's when we went on our Girls' weekend. At last. Aunt Eira said it could still be to New York City. Just her and me.

No, I said. That's not what I really want. The three of us – my aunt, me and my best friend – went to Montreal instead. Sam tried to beg off, but I talked her into coming.

We did a city tour and went shopping and to the Museum of Fine Arts. We went to the Barbie Exhibit, because Aunt Eira said she's always wanted to see it. We searched for the very best Montreal bagel, the very best place to get pastries and the very best hamburger. We rode on the Metro (that's the subway) and went rock climbing at Allez Up and to the Planetarium and to see *Phantom of the Opera*.

It was fantastic! So much fun, all of it. I wish we could live in Montreal and do all those things all the time! But Aunt Eira said, "Never mind. I'm sure we'll be going back!"

Sam and I bought dresses to wear to Aunt Eira's wedding – we're going to be two of the Women of Honour. I also bought a fairytale book for Daisy, a bunny toy for Lily and a ukulele for Uncle Gus. And art supplies for me.

We helped Aunt Eira choose her dress, which is more of a summery flowery kind of dress than just a regular white wedding dress. And we found a sweet summer dress the colour of orange sherbet – Daisy calls it the ice cream dress – for mum.

The Happy Paws are going strong, with four groups now in Seabright and near here, in Brighton, New Minas and Canning. They have taken over making and selling all the friendship bracelets and they also sell some of our cookies and bars and art cards I make. They're doing great. I'm really proud of them and of myself, for helping get them started.

Mo is a pretty good cookie-maker, but they've decided after working at the café this summer, what they really want to do is go back to school to become a teacher, like their uncle, Mr. Cadeau. Mo's hoping to get into Acadia University, because it's here and they wouldn't have to move. Plus, they'll still be able to work part-time at our café.

Mom and Aunt Eira and Uncle Dom promoted Sheila to kitchen manager and hired Hannah to manage the café and the bed and breakfast.

I no longer do volunteer work at Sunflower Pet Rescue Shelter. I just have so little time now. I do help with the rescues at Jayden's, any time I can.

Uncle Gus hasn't even got all his condos and apartments finished, but they're all either sold or rented. I think he saved the best one for us. He says we can move in anytime we're ready.

I pulled out that mess of a bride's crown and took another look at it. And decided, maybe it's not that bad, after all. I think I can make it work in time to give to my aunt.

Mum decided to save her beauty day gift with Mo for when she's getting ready to go to Aunt Eira's and Uncle Dom's wedding. Then, she started to lose her hair from the chemotherapy. Mo came over and shaved it off for her, because it was too upsetting seeing it come out in clumps every time she washed her hair or brushed it.

We came back from the Girls' Getaway with these beautiful silk scarves we found at the vintage shops in Montreal. Mo and Mum experimented with how to wear them as headscarves.

I drew a picture of my mother, in the prettiest of these scarves. It's all golds and oranges and a bit of red. I did it in colour. I framed it and gave it to Mo, to say thank you. I made a copy of it to give to my father. Some day.

I bought myself an easel, a seriously real one, not the kind kids get for finger-painting. If I'm going to be a serious artist, and I am, I decided I need serious tools.

Gus wrote a song about me. He calls it, *The Girl Who Saved My Life*. It's not a silly song. It's more of a ballad. But you wouldn't slow-dance to it. And that's another secret that got told, at last. Gus used to be a musician. He sang or played piano or sometimes drums on a lot of rock star's albums. He played some of the songs where Anne Murray or Gordon Lightfoot or Neil Young is singing and he's one of the people playing in the background. They all sound pretty good to me. He says he never got famous, but he did write lots of songs, including one that DID get famous, for a while. That was a million years ago or so, he says, back in the 1970s.

"Yeah, we all wanted to be the Beatles or the Rolling Stones, back then," he says, and laughs. "But I guess I did OK out of it." That's because he earns money every time somebody else records one of the songs he wrote or plays it on the radio or samples it in their own music. I had no idea this is how music works. It was so interesting when Gus explained it to Sam and me.

He records himself doing his song about me and Dom helps him put it up on YouTube and the crazy thing is, it gets a lot of likes and shares. Really a lot. Like decades after he just walked away from having his song get famous maybe he'll get to be famous all over again.

Maybe I'll get to be famous, too, as an artist.

And Sam will be famous as a musician. And composer.

And Jayden will be as well, for breeding and training racehorses.

Our family will have a successful business, the café.

We'll have a new home, at Sea Garden.

My mother will get better. She says she's trying, really hard. I know she will.

My father. Uncle Dom and Aunt Eira have said they'll help me find him. I know I will.

As Uncle Gus always says, "Anything could happen!"

the end

Want to know what happens next for Morley Star, her family and friends?

Sisters is the next book in this series. It will be published late Spring, 2022.

In it, Morley finally finds her father... and another big secret her mother has kept is revealed. It all starts when a mysterious teenager comes to the door, looking for a place to stay ...

Find out more about Sisters and the whole Morley Stories series at: www.CrimsonHillBooks.com

If you'd like to get an email reminder when Sisters is published, write to Jacquelyn at crimsonhill.net and put More about Morley in the Subject line.

About the Author

Jacquelyn Johnson writes books for curious and creative kids ages 8 to 12.

She used to work as a newspaper and magazine writer and editor. Her articles and photographs have appeared in newspapers and magazines in Canada, United States and Britain.

Jacquelyn is also a former teacher, college and university lecturer. She has taught English as a Second Language to children and teenagers in South Korea and journalism to university students in South Dakota and Ontario.

When not writing, she enjoys watching her garden grow while doing as little actual garden work as possible, re-decorating her home with shabby chic finds (that means fixed up used stuff, a hobby she shares with Morley's mother, Eefa) and music.

She grew up studying piano and later played the trumpet, though regrets that she has never learned to play as well as Sam Park. Or make jewellery as well as Morley. Or ride horses, like Jayden can.

She makes her home and garden with her family near the ocean in a town very much like Seabright. Just down the street from a house that's very much like Morley's. With a little cat who's very much like Feather.

Acknowledgements

If you've gotten all the way to this end of the book, you've already spent some time with Morley, Sam, Jayden and their friends and families. Thank you – it is a true delight to hear about readers of all ages enjoying these stories and their time in the Morley world.

Even though there's only one person's name on the cover, in fact no book could exist without many people contributing in many ways. Some of the people I send out heartfelt thanks to are:

Les Emmerson, the song composer, band singer and front man of Five Man Electrical Band. He wrote many songs, one of which was briefly a big hit, but he earned royalties from that one hit for decades. He is the real-life inspiration behind the 'secret' musical life of Morley's Uncle Gus.

My sister Janice Showman gave me the 'anything can happen' idea – so perfectly what Gus would say, so he does.

My sister Cathy Kaufman is the one who inspired the countdown idea – so perfectly a Morley thing.

Tammy Skater and David Skater, whose The Real Scoop ice cream shop in Wolfville, Nova Scotia gave me the inspiration for Scoops. Tammy's and David's hand-made ice cream is phenomenal (sometimes doing research really is this delicious!).

Eva's Café is something like Essentially English Bakery, not far from Seabright in Hantsport, Nova Scotia if you combined it with Frannie's Mini Donuts in Sanford, Maine. They are each different, unique, and worth a visit!

The need to wait out bad times Eira recalls from a British detective show is a quote from DCI Fred Thursday (portrayed by Roger Allam) on the third episode, Season 8 of the brilliant ITV series *Endeavour*.

Thank you to my husband and life partner Wayne for insights and drawing the plans for how to turn a red-brick elementary school into stylish new homes. And just about infinite support, encouragement and chicken dinners.

Thank you to our son, Jesse, for book design and formatting.

In memory of Timothy Billotte, the friend we lost while this story was coming into being. He inspired Gus' workshop, as well as Gus' kind and easy-going nature. It was Tim, a special friend who was an usher at my wedding, who made the jewellery boxes with inlaid fossils. We miss him.

I'm grateful to CBC Radio 2 who, from 9 a.m. to 3 p.m. each weekday, play the soundtrack to this series.

And thank you to Morley, who walked into my life one day and changed it forever when she insisted I tell you her stories.

Seabright is a small university town on the Fundy shore of Nova Scotia, not unlike the little town I live in, full of people who hunker down in winter but welcome visitors and guests in summer to relax and enjoy the sea views, excellent seafood and local wines as well as the gardens, hiking, tide-surfing, whale-watching and looking for fossils on the beaches. Or simply indulging in the laid-back lifestyle of this sweet corner of the world.

Perhaps, one summer soon, you'll be able to join them? But beware – you may find yourself so relaxed, and enchanted, you just can't bring yourself to ever leave …

Jacquelyn Johnson

January, 2022

CPSIA information can be obtained
at www.ICGtesting.com
Printed in the USA
LVHW020542111122
732651LV00009B/743